REQUIEM FOR
AN OUTLAW

Other Books by Terrell L. Bowers

Crossfire at Broken Spoke
Destiny at Broken Spoke
Feud at Broken Spoke
Judgment at Gold Butte
Konniger's Woman
Noose at Sundown

REQUIEM FOR AN OUTLAW

•

Terrell L. Bowers

AVALON BOOKS
NEW YORK

Published by Avalon Books,
an imprint of Thomas Bouregy & Co., Inc.
New York, NY

Library of Congress Cataloging-in-Publication Data

Bowers, Terrell L.
    Requiem for an outlaw / Terrell L. Bowers.
        p. cm.
    ISBN 978-08034-7400-0 (hardcover : acid-free paper)
    I. Title.
    PS3552.O87324R46 2012
813'.54—dc23

                                            2011040005

PRINTED IN THE UNITED STATES OF AMERICA
ON ACID-FREE PAPER
BY RR DONNELLEY, HARRISONBURG, VIRGINIA

For my daughters, Melanie and Nicole,
who added love, beauty, and charm to my life

Chapter One

Latigo Dykes dragged the small tree over to block the trail and paused, hands on his hips, arching his back to relieve the stiffness.

"Getting too old to be cutting and dragging trees around, Latigo," he muttered aloud. "And that's the gospel truth."

He shook off the weariness and took up his position. Buck Ellington was driving the stage today—no strongbox this trip—which meant no guard, and there were only three passengers. He knew Buck always drove with a shotgun at his feet, but he had never tried to shoot it out with anyone. The driver knew his life was worth more than the few dollars that might be in the mail sack, and the passengers were an elderly couple and a gambler.

Always a man who planned meticulously, Latigo lifted his Colt Frontier as he heard the approach of the wagon.

Buck slowed down to cross at the bottom of the gully, so there was no difficulty stopping the team when he confronted the blockage on the trail. Latigo was poised and ready. Buck yanked back on the reins, seeing the tree in their path, and shouted "Whoa!" at the horses.

Rising up from his position, Latigo kept his hat down to hide the upper portion of his face, and a silk bandanna was pulled up over his nose to hide the lower portion. He pointed the pistol at the driver.

"Hey there, Buck!" he called out. "Don't be doing anything heroic. I'm not intending to cause anyone harm."

"Damn it all!" Buck snarled. "You stopped me last week over at Billy Goat Wash. This is getting to be a habit."

"I do beg your pardon, Buck, but I only need one slight inconvenience, and I'll let you be on your way."

"What is it this time?" Buck wanted to know. "That banker, Nathan Hawks, wanted the company to fire me because I let you rob him last time. He claimed you had robbed him a couple months before."

"I only took what he stole from some poor farmers. He was out to steal their land and resell it for a pile of money. He's lucky I left him enough money to keep right on robbing more of those unfortunate people."

"He vowed he would use every dime he had left to find you and kill you," the driver warned.

"He can try."

"What's this . . . the fifth time you've stopped me in the past two years?"

"You are one of my favorite people, Buck," Latigo told the driver. "Now, if you would be so kind, please step down and trot out your passengers." As the man set the brake and hooked the reins around the handle, he added, "And make sure none of them get rambunctious. You know I'm not a violent man. I would sorely hate to shoot someone just to save my own life."

Buck climbed down and opened the passenger door. "Light down, folks," he instructed the three people inside the coach. "No tricks and this will be over in five minutes or less. There's no need for concern; just do what the Gentleman Bandit tells you to do."

"Dear me, Harley," a woman's voice exclaimed. "It's the famous robber!"

"We'll do like he says, Mama," her husband replied. "The Gentleman Bandit has never hurt anyone."

The three piled out and formed a line with the driver. Latigo approached with the gun still aligned at the group. He gave a nod to the elderly couple. "You folks can get back on the stage, though I'd appreciate it if you didn't pull a gun or try something that might get someone hurt."

"See, Mama?" Harley spoke softly to his wife. "It's just like I told you."

"Wait till the kids hear about this!" the woman said breathlessly. "They won't believe it!"

Latigo waited until they were in the coach to address the gambler. He had been at the saloon and watched him at the poker table last night. The man made his living at cards, but he wasn't content to play the odds. As Latigo did a lot of gambling himself, he quickly recognized a professional and knew most of the tricks.

"I know the sort of man you are," Latigo said.

The man glowered at him, his teeth bared in a sneer. "Yeah, well, I'm the sort of man who would like to put a hole in your gut."

"You were the big winner at poker last night," Latigo

said, ignoring the man's threat. "I suspect you took the other four at the table for several hundred dollars."

"Can't fault me for being a better player than any of them," he boasted.

"Not a better player, but a superior cheat," Latigo countered. "You palmed a good many cards during the night, and I'll allow that you deal the bottom card as clean as anyone I ever saw. Those skills give a man a considerable edge on most hands."

"Now, wait a minute, you! I don't like—" He stopped midsentence as Latigo leveled his gun at the man's head.

"You don't like what?" Latigo asked. "That I recognize a cardsharp and a cheat when I see one? Or is it because you're going to split your ill-gotten gains with me?"

"I'm just saying those guys shouldn't play if they can't afford to lose their money."

Latigo hardened his voice. "Maybe so, but they ought to have an even chance at winning. Plus, you've a nasty way of pushing a sucker into losing more than he can afford. I know a little something about that."

"Most men who gamble are sheep looking to be fleeced. If I didn't take their money, someone else would."

"Open your cash pouch and count out your poke. I'll take half and leave you half. That's more than fair, considering you wouldn't have won a lot of those hands if you hadn't cheated."

The gambler swore under his breath. "One day someone is going to find out who you are and put you in the ground."

"Not today, tinhorn. Start counting."

The gambler pulled out a leather wallet and began to

sort out his money. The dollar amount came out even, and Latigo moved up and took half. Then he backed away and ordered the man to help the driver move the felled tree from the road. When both men were busy with the chore, Latigo disappeared into the brush, grabbed up his horse, and was quickly up a wash and over the hill.

"You were durn lucky again today, Lat," he said aloud. "One of these days you're going to run into someone who will pull his gun. It will be kill him or be killed. You don't want to stay in this business until that happens— and that's the gospel truth."

It was not an enviable position for Wes Gavin. As a deputy U.S. marshal, he had had the misfortune of capturing Jay Quinteen for murder. The man was found guilty and hanged. His death did not sit well with his outlaw family. They had sworn vengeance against Wes, and they were men of their word.

The marshal wanted Wes to get out of town, to lay low until he and the other deputies managed to capture the rest of the gang. Wes had to smile, thinking of the size of that chore. Jay had ridden with his father, two brothers, his uncle and two sons, plus whoever else was in the Quinteen gang. He might as well pick up his gear and head for Alaska. As it turned out, he had a second option. A longtime nemesis of his, one whom Wes had tried to catch on several occasions, had held up a stage over near River Bend, Colorado. Rather than go into hiding, he took on the rigorous task of trying to run the elusive robber to ground.

The bandit was unusual in a number of ways. He was

the only man Wes had gone after and never managed to catch. He would disappear for weeks or even months between holdups, and no one seemed to have a decent description of the man. He usually robbed a stage, a businessman, or someone traveling alone, but he never took anything from a woman or from any of the impoverished passengers. Plus, when he committed a robbery, he always left the victim a portion of his money. He made a point of targeting gamblers, bankers, or shady businessmen, but he never took enough to ruin an individual. He was polite, never resorted to threats—other than the pointing of a gun—and he had never hurt anyone.

All of his gentlemanly acts did not settle accounts for being a highwayman. He was a bandit, a thief, a criminal. He had gotten away with his trade for a good many years, and it was high time someone brought him to justice. Wes intended to be that man.

Days wore into weeks, but Wes finally picked up the scent. From the valleys of western Colorado to the mountain range above the Cimarron River, he stuck to the running outlaw like a sand burr to a saddle blanket. Finally, in the shadow of the palisades of the San Juan range of mountains, his doggedness was rewarded.

It was early afternoon when he spied a saddled horse. The mount had come up lame, and the rider was not to be seen. Wes eased his horse forward carefully, his rifle cocked and ready. Although the outlaw had never shot or killed anyone, the Gentleman Bandit might turn violent to avoid capture. A bullet to eliminate his pursuer might seem preferable to spending a number of years behind bars.

Wes paused in the saddle, his horse standing perfectly still, while he used his keen sense of hearing and listened for any sound that didn't belong in the rugged region of the San Juan Mountains.

The wind was calm, the sunny day comfortably warm. A bird chirped from a short way off, and there was a rustle of leaves in a nearby undergrowth as a chipmunk scurried to its hole. The horse he had followed for several days was no longer part of the hunt. The footprints showed that, trapped within the box canyon, the man had headed up toward a maze of towering rocky buttes. If he continued his way back into the high sierras, he would be hard to find. However, it wouldn't do for Wes to leave his horse unattended. The bandit might find a way to circle back and . . .

Wes smiled to himself.

Nudging his horse along the path taken by his prey, he continued along until he reached the base of the rocky escarpment. He couldn't take the horse up the steep mountainside, so he tied him off to a branch of a nearby cedar tree. Then he studied the numerous crags and sheer, precipitous pathways. He began to climb, able to follow the man's flight from where the rocks and dirt had been disturbed by the fugitive's climbing. The scuff marks went up between two house-size boulders, which stood like sentries to the many cliffs and mountains beyond. Surrounded by weathered quarry face and patches of shale rock, there were only one or two ways the man could go.

Wes hurried along, sticking to the man's trail, grunting from the difficulty of the climb. Working his way up the near-vertical incline, he stuck to the path left by the bandit, disregarding any fear of ambush. After a considerable distance, he made a sharp turn and went over a knoll to a gully. He dropped down into the ravine, quickly reversed his direction, and returned quietly back down to where he could watch his horse.

Waiting in the tranquil mountain air, Wes could hear only his own breathing. Then, after a few minutes, there came a slight scraping sound of boots on a slick portion of rock. Wes risked a peek and spied the bandit edging over the rounded top of a smooth stone crown, a conical rock formation some fifteen feet above the valley floor. He appeared to be searching the terrain, trying to figure out where his pursuer had gone.

But Wes had guessed the man would make a false trail, keep hidden, and then sneak past him and try to steal his horse. He was ready, his rifle pointed up at the outlaw, as the man moved out into full view.

"You've nowhere to go, mister!" he shouted. "Toss your gun and come on down!"

The bandit had risen to a standing position, leaning over the very rim of the rock facade, trying to get a look at the waiting horse. He whirled about to scramble for cover, but his feet went out from under him, and he fell onto his stomach. Because of the severe slope of the perch, he began to slide backward. He used both hands, clawing for a handhold, but the stone surface had eroded until it was nearly smooth. There was nothing to cling to, and he skidded helplessly over the short cliff's edge.

Wes held his breath—there was nothing he could do. The man tumbled from the spindlelike roost and landed on his back with a grunt. Wes scrambled over the rough, uneven ground until he reached the bandit. He saw that the man's eyes were closed, but he appeared conscious. Wes stood over him, gun pointed right at his chest, and smiled over his victory.

The man rolled his head from side to side and gulped in a swallow of air. When he opened his eyes, he was looking into the muzzle of a gun. He uttered a groan of dismay and slowly rose up onto his elbows.

"Fall like that would kill most men half my age," he complained, continuing to work himself up into a sitting position. "Best be thankful I'm a tough old codger, or you'd have a busted-up or dying prisoner to take care of."

"You're the one who ought to be thankful," Wes retorted. "There are a lot of leaves and soft soil in this hollow. Otherwise you'd have broken your neck."

"You fall fifty feet and then tell me how soft the soil is," the man lamented.

"Fifty feet would have killed you," Wes corrected him. "It's not more than twelve to fifteen feet from where you actually came off the rock to the ground."

The old gent snorted his contempt. "Story sounds better at fifty feet. Can't have people saying the Gentleman Bandit had the wind knocked out of him from any shorter fall than that."

Wes uttered a sigh of resignation. "All right, to preserve your dignity, we'll call it fifty feet."

The wanted man squinted up at him, blinking at the sun shining from over Wes' shoulder. "You're the same jasper who tracked me for a month or more last year."

"Before you went into hiding," Wes allowed.

"I never take more than I need to live . . ." His lips curled into a wry grin as he added, "Comfortably."

"Well, I've got to admit, you're the hardest man I've ever had to catch," Wes said. "It wasn't only last year I came looking for you. I've been after you on and off for the better part of three years, ever since I started wearing a badge."

"What were you before—a bounty hunter, a scout for the Army?" he wanted to know. "I ain't never had anyone stick on my back trail the way you have. You're part bloodhound—and that's a fact."

"I could take that as an insult about my parents, but I'll let it pass. Can you stand up?"

The gent gave it some effort, but when he attempted to rise up to his feet, he collapsed back to a sitting position on the ground.

"By Hannah!" he grumbled. "I reckon I'm getting old and frail. Fall from a lousy hundred-foot-high ledge, and I still ain't got my strength back." He lifted his arm enough to see a scrape near his elbow that had bled some. "And I bruise a mite easier too."

Wes sighed over the exaggerated distance of the fall. As he didn't completely trust the old boy not to try something, he didn't offer to lend him a hand. "Remove your gun belt and try again."

"Worried I might get the drop on you, youngster?"

"I'm not convinced you are as shaky as you let on."

He laughed at that. "Oh, yeah? When is the last time you fell off a hundred-and-fifty-foot cliff? I got a right to be a little shaky."

"The gun," Wes ordered again.

The bandit removed his pistol and belt and passed them over to Wes. He then got his feet under him and gingerly rose to a standing position. He tested his legs and arms, as if making certain nothing was broken. When he looked at Wes, he put a grim expression on his face.

"Who are you?"

"I am deputy United States marshal Wes Gavin."

"Well, Marshal, you might not believe it, but I'm glad you finally caught up with me." The words were spoken wearily. "I'm too old to keep running and hiding. That stage holdup was going to be my last. I only had one more thing to do before I died, but like every other mistake I've made in my life, I've gone and messed that up too."

"Time's a-wasting," Wes said. "Let's get a move on."

"Going to be real hard on your horse, packing double," the outlaw observed thoughtfully. "Maybe you ought to just forget about me and leave me here. I can't be going anywhere without a horse, so I'll likely perish in a few days."

"We'll manage, old-timer. If I have to carry you on my back, you're going to stand trial for your crimes."

"You sound a mite on the touchy side, Marshal. Did I take money from your kin or a friend of yours?"

"Not that I'm aware of."

"You're doing your job here, and I don't hold it against you. I made a living taking what wasn't rightly mine, and I always expected to pay for that one day. But I hate having anyone think bad of me."

Wes was dumbfounded. "Think bad of you?" he cried. "You're a robber, a bandit, a highwayman!"

"I never shot or hurt anyone . . . and I never left them broke. I took what I needed from scoundrels and cheats. I'm a bandit, I admit that, but I'm not a bad sort. I've given money and food to starving families; I helped a couple men save their farms; I once paid a debt so a fellow wouldn't be beaten or maybe killed and leave his wife and child behind; I even donated money to get an honest man elected to the post of sheriff one time.

"As for you, I've had a hundred chances to waylay you along the trail. I could have slipped into your camp last night while you were sleeping down by the creek and cut your throat." He clucked his tongue. "I caught a fish for my breakfast not a hundred feet from where you were bedded down." He paused to scratch his head. "Thinking on it now, I should have swapped horses with you. Mine coming up lame was how you managed to catch up with me."

Wes scrutinized the man, wondering about his wild tales. Could there be any truth to his ridiculous stories? He decided it didn't matter and motioned for him to walk over to his waiting horse.

"Let's wrap a bandage on your arm and get going, old-timer."

"I go by Latigo Dykes," the man said. "I might be along in years, but I don't enjoy being referred to as an old-timer."

"All right, Latigo." Wes used his name. "We'll strip that nag of yours, so she can fend for herself, and get moving."

"I appreciate the concern for my horse, Marshal." He was practically chipper. "Mind if we take along my saddlebags? I have everything I own in them except for the clothes tucked into my bedroll."

"It's going to be a load on my horse just packing you."

"I'm not all that much for weight, Marshal. And you don't have to worry—I'll do whatever you say."

Wes couldn't see so much as a hint of deceit in the fellow's makeup. Perhaps the Gentleman Bandit was telling the truth about being relieved that his life of crime was over.

Chapter Two

Ogden Van Ness stood firm. "We've discussed this before," he told his son. "I need you to manage the ranch. I can't do all the work myself."

"I'm sick and tired of tending cattle, Pa," Glen battled back. "Why should Cousin Axel get to run a saloon, while I'm riding herd on a bunch of stinking cows?"

"Because his father—my brother—Logan, is the one who built the saloon. When he died, the business naturally went from father to son. Besides which, he is five years older than you, and he's married with a child on the way. He's a more stable influence for the saloon than you would be."

Glen swung his head around as if it was on a swivel. "Ever since Matt died, I get all the dirty, smelly jobs."

"Matt spoiled you," Ogden argued back, "always letting you run off and play or fool around." He put his hands on his hips and glowered at Glen. "It's time you learned to be a man and stand on your own two feet. I put you in charge of thirty men and a thousand head of cattle. What more do you want?"

"To have some fun," he replied tersely. "To drink, gamble, and spend time carousing with women. I want some time off so I can party all night long and sleep till noon the next day. All I ever get to do is stay here on the ranch and work."

"A man has to accept responsibility to become a man," Ogden pointed out. "You have to earn your own way in this world."

"Promote someone else to be the ranch manager," he whined. "You've already got Emmett as the foreman. He can do 'most everything I do. Why put the entire load on my shoulders?"

"I built this ranch from the ground up. My brother and I started this town. We worked side by side for ten long years to get a foothold in the middle of this wilderness. We fought Indians and cold and—"

"Yeah, yeah, I've heard it all before," Glen cut him off, showing his boredom by raising both hands in surrender. "Well, I ain't you, I ain't Uncle Logan, and I ain't my big brother."

Cleo entered the room to catch the last of his statement. She giggled, always eager to take her year-younger brother down a notch. "Keep going, Glen," she challenged. "When you come to *I ain't even a man*, I'll back you up 100 percent."

"Nobody asked you to butt in, dog puss!" he snarled at her. "You take a free ride on this here ranch. The only thing you do is take up space."

"Not all of it," she fired back in sharp retort. "There's plenty of space between your ears." She laughed derisively. "We could run a fair-sized herd of cattle on those wide-open plains."

"You're real funny, sis—funny like apoplexy," Glen retaliated.

"That's enough!" Ogden cut off their bantering. "This was a private conversation between me and Glen. If you want to make a nuisance of yourself, Cleo, go bother your mother."

"She sent me to fetch you two bickering children for breakfast."

"I ain't sticking around," Glen snapped. "I'm taking a break from work and heading into town."

"We've got branding to do!" Ogden objected.

Glen curled his lips in a sneer. "Let little Miss Wiseacre handle the iron. She can probably talk the calves into branding one another. As for me, I'll be back when I'm durn good and ready."

"Glen!" Ogden bellowed. "You walk out that door and I'll . . ."

But his son was already gone, slamming the front door behind him.

There were a few moments of awkward silence before Cleo spoke up. "I didn't mean to make trouble, Daddy," she said quietly. "I thought Glen would get to joking and cussing me like always."

"It isn't your fault, daughter," Ogden said soberly. "I let Matt carry the load for too many years. He didn't mind doing all the work while Glen tagged along without any responsibility. When he took ill . . ." He had to swallow a lump that rose in his throat. "Well, we never expected he would pass and leave so many duties for Glen."

"It was that dastardly pneumonia that took him," Cleo murmured gently. "I miss him too."

Ogden moved over and put his arm around his daughter. She leaned in close and offered up a bright smile, always happy to receive attention from him.

"So who has been around trying to court you lately?" he teased, dismissing his hurt and disappointment concerning Glen. "I haven't had to chase off any suitors in the past few weeks. Don't tell me you've gone through every eligible man in the valley?"

"Not quite," she chirped. "There's still a couple locals I've yet to look over, and more eligible men come through town every week. Don't worry, Dad, I'll find one who measures up one of these days."

"Let's have some breakfast. I'll give your brother a day or two to get rid of some of the mustang in his blood. Then I'll bring him back and put him to work. I'll make a man out of him if it kills him."

"Kind of loses the sense of purpose if you kill him," Cleo quipped.

Ogden chuckled, his daughter making his mood lighter. "I see why you don't have any serious suitors—no one can manage your wit."

"You think men are intimidated by a girl who might be smarter than they are?"

"A truly smart woman knows that the way to get a man is to hide her intelligence until she has her brand on him. Then she can rule the roost."

"Is that the way Mom got you to the altar?"

"What did she tell you?"

Cleo displayed a wholly innocent expression. "Oh, she has always claimed you're the one with the brains in the family."

He laughed. "Now you know how she landed me for a husband."

She laughed with him, and they headed for the dining room.

Two men suddenly burst out from behind a stand of trees and caught Wes unaware. He was under their guns by the time he stopped his horse. Latigo had been half-asleep behind him, and he grunted at the sudden halt.

"By Hannah, youngster!" he piped up. "You fall asleep too, or did . . . ?" Then he spied the two men.

"Buster . . ." Wes said to the man who blocked his path, "and Butch . . ." to the other, who was to one side. He had only seen the two men one time, but all the Quinteens had shaggy, rust-colored hair and a wealth of freckles. Add billy-goat teeth and angular faces—they were a homely lot. "You boys should have been out of the country by now. You know every lawman this side of Texas is looking for your gang."

"We had something to do first." Buster sneered the words. "You done killed our brother."

Wes looked around, but it appeared there were only the two men. Their cousins, father, and uncle were nowhere to be seen. "I only arrested him," Wes said carefully, his heart pounding hard enough to crack a rib. "A judge and jury were responsible for Jay's fate."

"Two slices from the same loaf of bread," Butch said.

"You might as well have put the noose around his neck yourself." He motioned for Wes to lift his hands.

Rather than drop the reins, Wes kept them tightly in his left hand and raised his arms. He watched for the slightest chance, but the guns of the two men were both aimed at his chest. The Quinteen boys were here to kill him. Somehow, they had gotten on his trail and followed him to the box canyon. They must have been familiar with the place and knew he would have to ride back the way he had gone in. They had waited, and now he was about one second away from being killed.

"Hey, boys," Latigo said cheerfully. "Am I glad to see you! This here law dog was taking me to jail. I'd have ended up spending the rest of my days behind bars. I'd find it right kindly if you would hold off shooting this fellow with me so close. I don't want to get killed along with him."

"You want to save your hide, Pops, slide down from the horse," Butch told him.

"I took a nasty fall off a fifty-foot cliff this morning," Latigo said, holding out his handcuffed hands so they could see the bandage around his arm. "I'm pretty stove up. How about one of you give me a helping hand down?"

"You can fall off or get shot," Buster sneered. "Your choice."

Latigo grinned. "I'll make a deal with you. Help me down and turn me loose; I'll make it worth your while."

"And how will you do that?" Butch asked.

"I've got some money stashed nearby. I'll pay you." The two brothers exchanged a quick look. "Fifty dollars and a gold watch, if you let me go and then let me have the marshal's horse. Mine came up lame. That's how he managed to nab me."

"If we shoot you, we'll take your money too."

Latigo laughed. "You don't know where to look. I knew this jackal was climbing up my back, so I buried my poke back down the trail a piece. It ain't far, but you wouldn't find it without my help."

"Maybe we could make you talk?" Buster threatened.

"I'm an old man, boys. If you try and beat the location out of me, I'll stonewall you until my dying breath." He let the words sink in and then said, "Letting me go will benefit us both."

Buster and Butch considered the offer, but their guns never wavered. Wes had no chance to try for his gun, especially with his hands raised.

"All right." Buster was the one to reply to Latigo's offer. "We'll take you up on the deal, old-timer. Butch, help the man down and get his cuffs off."

Latigo purposely bumped Wes in the middle of the back as he swung his body around. It felt like a signal for something, although Wes didn't know what.

Butch put his gun away, got down from his horse, and came over to help Latigo. The old man acted as if he would slide over the tail end of the horse. He started to scoot back as Butch reached up to help support his weight, and then he dug his heel into the horse's flanks.

The horse reared and jumped forward, bucking right into Buster's mount. Latigo both fell and was tossed off at the same time, landing on top of Butch. Wes jerked the reins to turn his pony into Buster's mount and plunged at him. The power of his horse's front shoulders slammed against the retreating, surprised horse under Buster. In its attempt to back away, the horse hit Butch's steed. The two animals bucked and kicked, lashing out at each other.

Wes ducked under Buster's gun arm, grabbed on to it with both hands, and used his leverage to pull him off his horse. Kicking free of his stirrups, he left the back of his mount and dragged Buster to the ground. Before the outlaw could scramble free, he clouted him two solid punches in the jaw and knocked him senseless.

Jerking his own gun from its holster, he whirled to meet Butch . . . only to see that Latigo had him pinned on the ground and had taken away his pistol. For a moment, he though the old boy might turn the gun his way. However, once Latigo saw that Wes had disabled his man, he tossed the pistol over at his feet.

"It's like I told you, youngster," he said solemnly, "I'm through running."

Wes dug into his pocket, removed a key, and flipped it to Latigo. "Take off your iron bracelets, Latigo. We'll shackle these two together, and they can double up on one of their horses."

The two brothers were soon handcuffed together and blaming each other for their change in fortunes. Wes kept them under his gun while taking a moment to speak to the Gentleman Bandit.

"You didn't have to throw in with me, Latigo. Once they killed me, those two would have likely let you go."

"I lied about burying any money. Besides that, I didn't want your death on my conscience."

"It would have been the Quinteen boys who killed me, not you."

"Yeah, but your death was something I could prevent. I did what I thought was right."

"You did more than that," Wes told him. "You helped me capture a couple of deadly criminals, both with fair-sized bounties on their heads."

"I don't see that a bounty will do me much good in prison," Latigo said, grinning. "After all, I'm your prisoner."

"It goes against my nature to simply let you go," Wes said. "But I sure enough owe you my life."

"Maybe we can strike a bargain," Latigo suggested. Wes eyed him narrowly, but he continued. "I need a small favor. If you can see clear not to turn me in right away, I know of a way you can pay me back."

"You need a favor?"

"It would take a few days is all, and maybe we can figure out how to put the reward for these two to good use."

Wes uttered a sigh. "I know I'm going to regret this, but what is the favor?"

Chapter Three

It was late afternoon when Wes slowed his horse at the edge of the town called Sunset. Latigo rode up alongside, leading the third animal with the Quinteen brothers aboard. They stopped for a moment, able to see a crowd gathered in front of the jail. Wes thought it was a mob but then discerned that most of the people were merely spectators. Three men dressed in cowboy garb—a large black man and two others—were facing a fourth, who was standing in the doorway to the jail. The one blocking the way had a shotgun in his hands, while the other three were spread out in a menacing manner, hands on their guns, as if ready to draw.

"Let me guess which man we came to help," Wes said sourly.

Latigo displayed a sheepish expression. "I haven't seen the boy in fifteen years, but that sure looks like him on the porch."

"You stay back with the prisoners while I sort this out," Wes advised, putting his horse into motion. He rode forward with purpose, drawing the attention of many in the crowd. The people parted at his approach, and Wes continued up to the jail, forcing two of the three men to move or be run over.

He ignored the grumbling trio and smiled at the very nervous-looking young man in front of the jail entrance.

"Howdy," Wes greeted him. "I'm looking for the local sheriff or marshal."

The man looked to be in his early twenties, with a face showing almost no tan. He cradled the scattergun in his left arm, and though he appeared fearful and uncertain, he stood his ground like a man.

"I'm Shep Donahue," he said nervously. "I work at the general store and also do the job of town sheriff when the need arises."

Wes gave him a nod and jerked a thumb over his shoulder in the direction of Latigo and his two prisoners.

"I've a couple of guests who need special lodging for a few days."

"Who do you think you are?" One of the trio of cowpunchers demanded to know. "You ride in here and butt into our affairs. You're looking to get stomped or shot full of holes."

"You tell him, Kip," the black man egged on his pal.

The third was a short fellow, and he also joined in. "Yeah, who does this joker think he is?"

Wes rested his hand on his gun and rotated in the saddle far enough to look down at the man called Kip. Instead of replying, he jerked the reins on his horse, turning the mount until his back was to the man. Using the heel of his boot, he gave a sudden jab to the horse's flanks. The animal immediately bucked forward and kicked back with both hooves.

One hoof caught Kip square in the chest and knocked him off his feet. Before the other two men could react, Wes whirled his horse back around and had all three of them under his gun.

"If it's trouble you boys are looking for, I can oblige you here and now." He kept his pistol moving back and forth between the two who were still standing, able to shoot either one if they made a grab for their gun. "I don't have time for this kind of foolishness, so draw down or lift your hands."

The two men both raised their hands, while Kip slowly rose to a sitting-up position, rubbing his newly bruised chest.

"We've no fight with you, mister," the large man said respectfully.

"That's right," said the short one. He swallowed hard and stared cross-eyed at the muzzle of the Colt .45. "We were only having some fun with Donahue."

"I've important business with the sheriff, boys," Wes announced. "Any of you object to my getting on with it?"

"No, sir. Hell, no!" the little man replied quickly. "We was just leaving."

Wes watched as the two men helped their pal to his feet. Then the three of them headed down the street toward a saloon. Seeing that the confrontation was over, the crowd began to break up. Most everyone started to walk away, except for a rather attractive, dark-haired girl. She had a pencil and notepad in her hand and was scribbling mightily.

Latigo neck-reined his mount past Wes and stopped at the hitching post. "These jaspers are wanted for a number of brutal crimes," Wes informed the town sheriff. "We need a place to put them until we can get a prison wagon. I have to contact the U.S. marshal in Denver for instructions."

"I have two cells," the man replied. "One is occupied at the moment, but you're welcome to put them in the empty one."

Latigo climbed down. "Give me a hand with these two polecats, sonny," he said to Donahue, "and I'll explain what's going on."

Wes dismounted too but waited until Latigo herded the two prisoners inside the jail before he stopped Donahue.

"We'll help you guard the prisoners until we get word back," he told him. "Looks like I interrupted a little trouble here too."

The acting sheriff gave a nod over his shoulder. "Those are friends of Glen Van Ness, my prisoner. They wanted me to turn him loose. I don't think it would have come to shooting, but I wasn't completely sure about that."

"Tough to cover three men when you are holding a gun with only two barrels of shot," Wes pointed out.

"I'm beholden to you for coming when you did. I've a wife and two kids. Hate to get myself killed and leave them on their own."

"Being a town sheriff isn't a great job for a family man."

"No one else would take the job, and I needed the extra ten dollars a month." He took a closer look at Wes. "Who are you, mister?"

"Wes Gavin, deputy U.S. marshal out of Denver. The two outlaws Latigo herded inside tried to bushwhack me this morning. They are part of the Quinteen gang and are upset over my arresting their brother, Jay Quinteen. He was hanged."

"The general store has a telegraph," Shep informed him. "I'm the telegrapher, but I can't leave my prisoner unattended."

"Once those two are behind bars, Latigo can watch the jail," Wes suggested. "I'll take the horses to the livery and meet you at the store."

"All right. I'll be along in a few minutes."

Wes gathered the reins of the three horses, but the young woman he had seen writing in a notebook moved quickly to block his path.

"I'm a reporter for the *Sunset Sentinel*," she said professionally. "May I ask you a few questions, Deputy Gavin?"

"If you're looking for a story, you pretty much overheard everything I told the sheriff. That was all the pertinent information about my being here."

"Yes, but you didn't say how you got here or where you were going when those two tried to ambush you. Is that man with you another deputy? What crimes are the two prisoners guilty of? You said their brother was hanged. What did he do?"

"Pull back on the reins, miss," he told her. "You're running me over with questions."

"Will you be staying here until we have a hearing for the murder suspect in jail?" she asked, changing the subject. "The killer is the son of a man who practically owns the town. As the judge is married to his sister, there's no way—"

Wes gave her an exasperated look, "Dad-gum, lady, could you stop talking long enough for *me* to take a breath?"

"My folks have allowed me to follow this story, and I need something new badly. Please," she said, displaying a persuasive enough plea that he would have given her the shirt off his back. "Won't you help me, Deputy Gavin?"

"Walk with me while I take these horses down to the livery," he offered. "You tell me what's going on here, and I'll see if I can answer a few questions."

She introduced herself as Dee Johnson. Her ink-black hair was tied back into a bun, her chocolate-colored eyes were bright with excitement, and she was about as cute as a baby chick in a hatbox.

"I was delivering a bundle of newspapers to the general store when Glen Van Ness road into town yesterday," Dee explained. "As I was leaving the store, I saw a man being tossed into the street in front of the Red Rose Saloon. He landed on his back and appeared to be dazed for a moment. I thought there might be a story in the works, perhaps a fight or some other drama I could write about, so I started to walk in that direction.

"Glen followed the man outside and stood over him. Then he called him a filthy, tinhorn sidewinder and yelled how he had warned him to stay out of town."

She took a breath and finished the story. "Well, the man rose up onto one elbow and swore at Glen. That's when Glen drew his gun and pulled the trigger!"

"Just like that?" Wes asked. "He killed him in cold blood?"

"Looked that way to me," she replied. "Shep heard the shot—he's the man you helped at the jail just now—and he arrested Glen."

"And that's it? There's nothing else you can tell me about the shooting?"

"Nothing, except for the gambler's pal checking to see how badly his friend was hurt. As soon as he saw his pal was dead, he left town. I guess he was afraid Glen might kill him too."

"He left before Shep had a chance to talk to him?"

"Yes, just checked his friend and then grabbed his horse and took off," she said. "Shep arrived after a couple minutes, and I happened to be the only witness to the shooting."

"What about the three men harassing the sheriff just now?"

"Those were some of Glen's pals from the ranch. They were trying to make Shep turn Glen loose."

"They didn't seem all that anxious for a fight."

"No, those three are mostly harmless, but it might have come to violence if you hadn't intervened." She gave a wave of her pencil. "It's all kind of silly too, because there is little chance Glen will be charged with any sort of crime." Wes frowned, and she explained. "The local judge, Samuel Stevens, is married to Glen's aunt."

Wes turned the animals over to the hostler. He set aside Latigo's saddlebags and removed his own war bag, so he would have his cleaning kit and a change of clothes.

Before he had time to look for a hotel, the girl was again in his face.

"Well?" she wanted to know.

"You want something to write in your newspaper—is that what you're after?"

"How refreshing to meet a man who doesn't miss the obvious," she exclaimed, undoubtedly piqued he had offered her nothing to this point. "Isn't that what I've been explaining to you at some length?"

He smiled at her indignation. "If you've got the nerve, I'll tell you what you can print so it will change things concerning the upcoming hearing."

That bit of news caused her to arch her eyebrows. "What are you talking about?" she asked.

"If the judge is related to the defendant, he can't ethically preside over the case. To demonstrate there is no bias, the case will have to be heard by a circuit judge, or there will have to be a change of venue to another town."

The girl was scribbling as fast as she could write. "You're claiming there's a law against a judge presiding over a case when he is related to the defendant?"

"It's the law of common sense. A judge is bound to be prejudiced when it involves his own bloodline."

"Jumpin' Jesse! This is great!" she cried. "You've been a big help, Mr. Gavin."

"Not at all, Miss Johnson."

"Really, this is going to be a great article!" she gushed, the excitement making her eyes flash like newly minted gold coins. "Thank you, thank you so much!"

He might have tried to speak to her about something

other than her story, but she spun about and took off at a run. It was entertaining to simply watch, as she had to lift her skirt to keep from stepping on the hem of her dress.

"I've put away all three animals for you." The stabler had come up behind Wes. "It's a dollar a day to stable three horses, plus two bits more each if you want me to rub them down."

"Sounds fair," Wes told him. "Give them a good going over. And I'll need a written bill when we leave town. Expenses for prisoners are reimbursed."

"Good thing you arrived when you did," he said. "Those Van Ness hands only have about one brain betwixt the three of them, but the standoff still might have ended in a fight. Hate to see young Shep get himself injured or killed."

"The man in jail must have some good friends."

"What he has is a father who owns most of this town and a large portion of the entire valley. He isn't going to want to see his boy go to prison for killing a tinhorn gambler."

"Sounds like you know the old man pretty well."

"My name's Joe Fremont," the man replied. "I'm married to one of Ogden Van Ness' two sisters. I believe I heard Dee tell you how Judge Samuel Stevens is married to his other one."

Wes introduced himself and asked, "What do you think? Any chance the shooting could have been self-defense?"

Fremont frowned. "Well, the newspaper gal stated

she didn't see a gun, and none was found on the body. I can't believe Glen would shoot a man in cold blood, but it don't sound good."

"You know anything about the dead gambler?"

"Yeah, him and his pal have been around a time or two before. They don't usually stay long because there aren't many people who will sit at their table. They seem to have a lot of luck playing cards," he finished meaningfully.

Wes filed the information away and asked, "Your brother-in-law, Ogden Van Ness, is he likely to take steps to help his son?"

"Ogden's older boy was a hell of a nice guy. He would lend a hand, fork over the price of a meal to a hungry family, or let a man borrow his favorite horse. Everyone liked Matt Van Ness. As for the young rooster, Glen has always been a troublesome sort. He drinks and gambles too much—ain't worth two hoots to his pa. It's a real shame it was Matt who died of fever instead of Glen." He shrugged his shoulders. "Course, I imagine Glen knows that's how people feel. It could be why he's more ornery now than when Matt was alive."

Wes absorbed what he had learned and asked, "Where can I get a room?"

"Over to the tanner's store. Wardle has a spare room around back of his place. Used to have his hired man living there until the guy got married last year and moved out. It's less noisy than the rooms over at the Silver Dollar Casino."

Wes thanked the man and began the short walk back to the jail. This little favor for Latigo could get dangerous real sudden. A powerful man's son in jail for murder? A store clerk as acting sheriff, one who was as green as spring grass, holding two vicious killers like the Quinteen boys for several days? Dad-gum, it wouldn't take much to turn this place into a graveyard.

Chapter Four

Emmett arrived right after breakfast and handed Cleo a copy of the *Sunset Sentinel*. She glanced at it for a minute, and he asked, "Don't look good, does it?"

Emmett was the ranch foreman, but he also ran errands and handled a lot of things Matt had once done. He was not exactly handsome, but Cleo thought he had a nice smile, and he always enjoyed a good laugh. He had tried to court Cleo for a time, but she knew they weren't suited for each other, and it never crossed into serious territory. He had recently been spending a lot of time with Dee Johnson. They would occasionally speak of the courtship, but Dee and Cleo didn't get along. As such, Emmett was usually careful as to what he told her.

"I still can't believe Glen would do something so crazy," she said, sticking to the business about her brother. "Kill a man in cold blood . . . For what? The paper said the gambler wasn't hurting anyone."

"I know he refused to talk to your father yesterday, and

then Kip, Scat, and Pepper tried to take him out of jail by force. Makes me wonder how this is going to end."

"Glen and Father had a row before he left the day of the shooting. I don't think either of them is going to bend enough to have a confidential chat."

"You see what Dee wrote today about your uncle?" Emmett asked, nodding at the paper. "He can't sit in judgment over your brother. A real judge will have to preside over the hearing. If there's a real trial, he'll sure enough get sentenced to prison—or worse."

Cleo stared back down at the page. "What?" She was shocked. "It says that?"

"Quoted from a visiting lawman, the same guy who rode in and stopped Kip and the others from trying to take Glen away from Donahue."

She shook her head, reading as fast as she could decipher the words. There hadn't been a school in Sunset until she was fourteen. She attended for almost two years but had done little more than learn to read at a minimal level.

"Right there," Emmett said, pointing. "See?"

"Pre—dis—position?" she sounded the word out with some effort. "And what does that and this other word, *bias*, mean?"

"It means your uncle would favor letting Glen get away with a murder. With that bit of news published in the paper, everyone in town knows there has to be a real trial."

"Daddy isn't going to like this."

Emmett grinned. "That's why I'm going to let you

take the paper to him. Do you need anything before I head out to the branding chutes?"

"Tell Raul to hitch me up the buckboard. Soon as I give this to Dad, I'm going to town and visit Glen. It sounds as if we may have to hire him a good defense lawyer."

"You mean you don't trust Wardle?"

She gave her head a negative shake, thinking of the local tanner who dabbled in writing contracts or settling minor disputes. "I might let him judge who had the faster horse in a race, but not defend Glen's life!"

"I'll help Raul get the buggy ready and have it in the front yard for you in ten minutes."

She said her thanks and was quickly into the house. Ogden was not going to be happy about the new turn of events. He had already decided there would be some local jail time, and perhaps a payment to the dead man's relatives, but this? Glen could end up being hanged for murder. Her father would never stand by and let that happen.

Before Cleo reached the kitchen, she heard the raised voices of her parents. She approached slowly, not wanting to intrude, yet she was close enough to overhear what was being said.

"It's not your fault." Her mother was speaking to Ogden. "I know you showed a little favoritism to Matt, but he was the oldest and a hard worker. I don't think for a minute that you are responsible for Glen shooting someone."

"I tried to give him the same love and discipline as Matt," Ogden lamented. "But I can't help being human. I'm bound to have made him feel less important than his brother. He was always trapped in Matt's shadow."

"It was Glen's way, Ogden," Naomi replied softly. "He was born headstrong and . . . well, it's probably my fault he didn't grow up as strong and responsible as Matt. I always tried to excuse his lack of ambition because he was the baby of the family."

The wooden floor creaked under Cleo's feet. As Ogden appeared in the doorway to the kitchen, Cleo made a quick stride forward, as if she had just entered.

"Emmett went to town early and brought by the newsletter," she explained, talking quickly to hide the immediate heat that was transferred to her cheeks. She hadn't been caught eavesdropping on her folks since she was concerned they wouldn't buy her what she wanted for her twelfth birthday. "It . . . it looks very bad for Glen," she continued. "Dee Johnson was standing less than a hundred feet away when Glen killed that stranger, and now it seems Uncle Samuel won't be able to preside over the trial."

The news she brought affected Ogden more than the thought of him and Naomi being overheard. He came forward and snatched the paper from her hand.

"Right there." Cleo pointed out the section written by Dee.

"What's it say, dear?" her mother asked, coming from within the kitchen to stand at his side.

"Just what Cleo said," he answered gravely. "Samuel won't be handling the case. A circuit judge will have to come into town for the hearing. It doesn't look good for Glen."

"He's going to need a good attorney," Cleo said.

"I'll write out a request for one to stand by and take it into town. I know a couple personally over in Denver."

"You needn't leave the ranch, Dad," Cleo offered. "I'm already having the buggy hitched up for me. I want to speak to Glen." He displayed a firm expression, so she quickly added, "He will be more likely to tell me what happened if you aren't along."

Ogden sighed in defeat, knowing her words were true. "I'll write the message, and you make sure Shep sends it off right away."

As he walked over to use a pen and paper, Cleo took a close look at her mother. There was a dread sadness in her face, and she appeared haggard and tired. The worry about Glen had taken a toll already. If he was to be imprisoned for a long term or possibly hanged . . . She shook the thought away before it could find a home in her consciousness. There was more to this than what the story stated in the newspaper. There had to be.

Wes entered the jail after a fair night's rest. Latigo and Shep were supposed to be taking turns watching the prisoners, but he found them both there.

"Thought you would cover for us for a spell," Latigo said to Wes. "Shep here invited me for breakfast and claims his wife is a great cook."

"Sure, you two go ahead," said Wes. "Get some sleep while you're at it. You can use my room, Lat, though it's probably more noisy during the day. I'll stick around the office till you return."

"What about your breakfast?"

"Don't worry about me, but you'd best pick up something for the prisoners before you desert me."

The two men left, and Wes was alone with the three prisoners. It didn't take long for Buster and Butch to start making noise. Their gang was going to find them, and then it would be too bad for Wes. He would rue the day he was born. He would die in a pool of his own blood. They would laugh and spit on him as the life left his body. It seemed the Quinteen boys had less than benevolent feelings for him.

"You two might want to be a little nicer to me," Wes warned, growing weary of their threats. "I control what you will eat until the prison wagon arrives." He grunted. "Even the buzzards won't touch what you will be getting once you leave here."

"Yeah, well, we ain't expecting nothing besides mush, bread, and water," Butch said. "You got to give us that much."

"Tell you what," Wes offered. "You two mind your manners when I'm around, and I'll see you get beefsteak for supper tonight."

Buster shoved Butch out of the way and eyed Wes with open suspicion. "Why would you do that?"

"I've nothing against you fellows," Wes replied. "About your brother, I only did my job when I arrested him. He didn't put up much of a fuss at the time, and we got along all right. Fact is, I was a little saddened when they pronounced the verdict. I didn't expect him to be hanged."

"You're still the man responsible for his capture!" Buster said.

"Like I said, it wasn't personal. You boys do right by me, and I'll see you get a good meal tonight."

They were mulling it over when the door suddenly opened. Wes had his back turned, paying attention to the Quinteen brothers. It was too soon for Latigo to have returned with breakfast. In self-defense, he spun about, and his gun flew to his hand, cocked—ready for instant use.

A girl had come through the doorway. Stunned by his violent reaction, she took an involuntary step back, missed the porch step, and sat right down on the dusty street!

Wes holstered his gun at once and hurried out to her. Her mouth was agape, eyes widened from shock, and a rush of crimson began to color her face from embarrassment. He reached down, took hold of her wrists, and quickly pulled her up onto her feet.

Recovering her wits, she swore softly under her breath and reached around, dusting off the back of her dress.

"Excuse me, miss, I didn't mean to—" He started an apology.

"Of all the stupid, boneheaded stunts!" she cut him off sharply. Then she visibly choked off further name-calling and demanded: "Do you greet all your guests by sticking a gun in their faces?"

Wes backed up a step and tipped his hat in a polite gesture. "I do beg your pardon, miss. You caught me by surprise."

"*You* were surprised!" she declared.

"Won't you come inside?" Wes invited, attempting to put the episode behind them. "And tell me what I can do for you."

She finished brushing off her dress, followed him into the office, and stopped to face him squarely. "I'm Cleo Van Ness. You have my brother in your jail."

"It's not my jail," he corrected. "I don't live in your fair town."

"You're guarding the place with your life," she countered sharply. "I'd say that makes it your jail."

"All right, but even if we agree this is my jail, your brother isn't my prisoner."

"He's behind bars, you are guarding the jail, that makes him . . ."

"Yeah, okay." He didn't allow her to finish. "It makes him my prisoner. I see how your logic works."

Glen sneered at his sister from his cell. "Did you come to banter back and forth with that two-bit lawman or to see me, Cleopatra?"

Wes smiled. "Cleopatra?"

The girl's cheeks reddened noticeably, and fires of anger leaped into her eyes. "I prefer Cleo," she snapped. "Especially from ill-mannered louts who go around pointing guns at anyone who walks through their door."

"You're right comely when you flare up that way, miss," he said, still displaying a grin. "Brings a sparkle to your eyes and color to your cheeks."

She bore into him with a heated gaze. "May I speak to my brother, or do I have to wait for Shep to return?"

Wes surveyed her with an all-inclusive glance. "You wouldn't try to pass your brother a weapon of some kind, would you?"

"Do you wish to search me?" was her haughty response.

He gave her a second look. "The idea sounds inviting,

but I don't think that will be necessary. I'm not in the habit of searching young ladies."

"Just pointing guns at them."

"I wasn't expecting a lady," he countered. "The two prisoners I brought in have friends who would have come into the jail shooting. That's the reason I reacted the way I did."

She glanced back at the Quinteen brothers. Both of them were on their feet, regarding her with the same disgusting leer.

Wes added, "I should have had the door locked, and then you would have had to knock. It would have saved both of us our pride."

The girl had composed herself, but the ire had not dissipated completely. "Perhaps I misjudged you," she said, not altogether ready to offer friendship. "You might not be an absolute oaf after all."

"Not the most endearing words I ever heard, but it beats being cussed at."

"Yes, well, you are fortunate I'm a lady and didn't use the words that came to mind."

He chuckled. "You're saucy enough to be named Cleopatra. And I've heard she was supposed to be an extraordinarily beautiful woman too."

The intended flattery rekindled the smoldering stare until it about singed his eyebrows. He quickly moved to one side and said, "You can visit for ten minutes, but don't get too close to the second cell. Those two outlaws would likely grab you and try to bargain their way out of here."

"It's a relief to know you're concerned for my welfare," she stated icily.

"Not at all," he replied with a grin. "If they escaped, I'd have a time of it running them down again."

Her repartee didn't miss a beat. "I take back the notion you might not be an oaf."

Wes chuckled at her spunk and allowed her to pass, closing the door and going over to sit behind the desk. He began to look over some handbills and wanted circulars, but he was able to overhear their conversation.

"Daddy wrote out a wire for me to send to retain the best attorney money can buy," Cleo informed her brother quickly. "I don't know how much help that will be. I read the report in the paper, and it said you killed the man in cold blood for no good reason. What were you thinking?"

Glen lowered his head shamefully. "I didn't intend to kill him, sis," he mumbled quietly. "The guy and his pal worked a table the last time I did some gambling. They were cheaters and took me for every dime I had. I was trying to scare him, run him out of town. When he pulled a hideaway gun"—he lifted his shoulders in a helpless shrug—"I was forced to shoot."

"The report Dee wrote said he didn't have a gun," Cleo stated.

"I saw it in his hand. He acted as if he was going to get up, but he snuck the small pistol out at the same time. He sure enough would have shot me."

"Why didn't Shep find a gun on him, then?"

"I don't know. Maybe his pal picked it up. I left him lying in the street. Next thing I know, Shep is taking my gun and herding me to jail."

"But you could hang, Glen! Don't you understand the seriousness of the charge against you? It's murder!"

Glen gripped the bars until his knuckles turned white. He pressed the top of his head against the steel rods, refusing to look at Cleo.

"Pa's been wanting me to act like a man. Looks like standing trial is the only way I can do this right," he said quietly. "As for you, well, you can believe it or not, but I only defended myself."

They passed a few more minutes talking back and forth, but Wes turned a deaf ear to the remainder of their dialogue. He allowed her fifteen full minutes before he spoke.

"Time is up, Miss Van Ness. You're welcome to come back this afternoon, but the inmates need to wash up for breakfast. It'll be here any minute."

She said good-bye to her brother and moved over to stand at the desk. "What do you think will happen to Glen?" she asked, this time using a polite tone of voice. "I mean, you are a genuine lawman, so I suspect you have seen a number of trials."

"It depends," he answered, aware of her deep concern but remaining truthful. "If the man did have a gun, it would be self-defense."

"Glen says he did."

"But the news gal and the sheriff say no gun was found on the body."

"His partner must have taken it."

"Find a way to prove that, and even if he started the fight and forced the man to draw, the most he would get is manslaughter. If the judge sees the shooting as cold-blooded murder, your brother could be sentenced to a good many years in prison or end up on the gallows."

Her eyes misted with helpless concern, but she sniffed back her tears. "Thank you for being honest and forthright, Marshal."

"The name is Gavin, Wes Gavin."

"Don't expect us to be on a first-name basis," she warned. "After all, you are holding my brother prisoner."

"Wrong," he corrected her. "I told you before, my prisoners are the two in the other cell. I have nothing to do with your brother being behind bars."

"Regardless, I have a rather low opinion of lawmen right now."

"Can't blame the man whose job it is to enforce the law, Miss Van Ness. The laws are here to protect us all."

"Of course." She lifted her chin and was purposely sarcastic. "I feel so much better knowing you are here to protect me."

"With my life, if need be," he said, with a cavalier tip of his hat. "And I mean that sincerely."

She paused to regard him thoughtfully. "I believe you do mean it."

"And I'm honestly sorry your brother got himself into a fix too," he added.

A frown furrowed her brow as Cleo took a step back and allowed her anger to subside. "It's a shame we are meeting under such dire circumstances."

"My first thought as well," he said, showing her his best smile. "I don't usually resort to pulling a gun on a lady and throwing a scare into her, just so I can help her back up onto her feet."

She almost smiled but held back. "Good day to you, Marshal Gavin."

"And to you too, Miss Van Ness."

She turned for the door as it opened. Latigo had a tray in his hands, carrying four bowls of oatmeal. He stopped dead in his tracks upon seeing the girl.

"Well, say!" he exclaimed. "It looks like I picked the wrong time to leave the office."

"Latigo Dykes, Miss Cleo Van Ness," Wes introduced. "Her brother is in the first cell."

"Had me going for a minute there," he said to her. "I was thinking the marshal here had found himself a pretty gal to court." The old boy winked. "However, I shouldn't think relatives of prisoners cotton much to lawmen."

"That's a point the lady and I covered right off," Wes remarked from behind the desk.

Latigo nodded in understanding but continued to regard Cleo with interest. "Well, don't you judge Deputy Marshal Gavin too harshly, little lady," he said in Wes' defense. "He might be a lawman, but underneath the badge and gun, Wes is a reasonably nice guy."

"Are you his deputy or his father?"

He laughed and backed out of her way. "Neither one." And when her look changed to one of curiosity, he replied, "I'm his prisoner."

Cleo about stumbled on the threshold a second time because of the man's odd remark. She managed to keep her feet this time and continued down the street. Latigo watched her admiringly for a moment or two before he entered the jail.

"Brought you some breakfast, along with the food for the prisoners," he told Wes, setting a bowl on the desktop.

"You're too kind, Lat." Then, with a stern look and speaking under his breath, he asked, "What are you trying to do, telling the lady you're my prisoner?"

"It's like I told you when you caught up with me. I've turned a new page on my life—no more lies."

"What about the reason we're here?"

"I'll deal with that once we get the reward in hand and have our two guests on their way to Denver to stand trial."

"And the case here in Sunset?"

"I've seen a couple reasons we might want to stick around until it's settled." He displayed a wry grin. "One of them just left the office."

"You thinking of getting me hitched to one of the local gals?"

"There's two fine-looking girls you've met since we arrived, and I'd wager you're one lonely deputy marshal. Why not mix some pleasure with business?" He moved over to the cells and handed out the three bowls of mush. When he came back to the desk, he set down the empty tray. "Now that I think on it, I recall seeing a notice of a town dance—for tonight too—over at the livery barn. Might give you a chance to check out one or both of those little fillies. You should attend that there shindig and see what hand fate deals you."

"There are likely a hundred men chasing after both of those young ladies," Wes told Latigo. "I don't think I stand much of a chance with either one."

"Go to the dance and test your luck," the old gent suggested. "You've got nothing to lose but your freedom."

"You'd better get some rest. It's going to be a long shift watching the jail this afternoon and tonight."

"Yeah, I hear you," he replied. "You can collect the empty dishes. I'll take them back to the café when Shep and I come back on shift."

Chapter Five

Ogden sputtered. "What kind of defense is that—the man went for a gun that no one else saw and no one can find?!"

"It's what he said, Daddy. He claimed the man had a gun and tried to shoot him, but by the time Shep arrived and checked the body, the gun was missing."

"What was the trouble to start with?"

"The gambler took his money last time he was in town. Glen claims he was a cheat. Now he said he is willing to do the honorable thing and stand trial."

"Bah! How honorable is it going to be if he ends up dangling from the gallows?"

"I believe him," she stated firmly. "Glen was the most serious I've ever seen him in my life."

"What's Shep got to say about all this?"

"I didn't see Shep. There was a Marshal Gavin at the jail."

"A marshal?"

"He has a couple of hardcase characters locked up in the cell next to Glen's."

"Did the marshal have anything to say?"

"Yes, he said Glen might get off with a couple years if the judge believed his story. Of course, it would be a big help to find out what happened to the gun."

"Where could the gun have disappeared to?" he demanded to know. "How can we help him if we don't know where to look?"

"Glen thought the dead man's pal might have taken it. He didn't tell me any more than that."

"Did you send off the wire I wrote out for that Denver attorney?"

"I left it at the store with Shep's wife. He was asleep. I guess he spent the night at the jail, him and another man."

"Shep hired a deputy?"

"No—and that's a bit odd too." At her father's curious look, she made a face to display her confusion. "He claimed to be a prisoner."

"Shep has someone in jail who is acting as his deputy?"

"No, the man arrived with Marshal Gavin. He said he was *his* prisoner."

"This makes no sense at all. I'm going to take a dozen men and—"

"No, Daddy!" Cleo said firmly. "We can't do things the old way anymore. I know you used to ride off and take justice into your own hands, but those days are gone. We have real law now, with courts and judges. You can't take action unless you wish to become an outlaw yourself."

He suddenly looked like a very old man. Old and

tired. "I can't sit by and watch my only remaining son be hanged."

"I'll go into the dance tonight and see what I can learn. If Shep isn't there, I can talk to him at the jail. Let me find out what I can about the chances of proving the gambler had a gun. I'll also see if there is any word back from the attorney."

"All right, Cleo," he acquiesced. "I'll let the law work for the time being. But if they decide to hang Glen, I'll be taking a hand."

She gave him a kiss on the cheek and hurried off to her room. She had a nice dress put away, but it might need some touching up. Plus she had to take a bath and wash her hair. She wanted to look special for the dance, and, despite the awkward circumstances, she could not deny an eagerness to see the marshal again.

Hyrum Quinteen sat his horse alongside his brother, Lark, and waited for his sons to arrive. Saul and Moab came up the draw and met them on the plateau. Their horses were covered in both dust and sweat from the hard riding.

"It's been two damn days! Did you see any sign of them—tracks, anything?" Hyrum asked his boys.

Saul shook his head and removed his hat. He began to fan his face with it. "Nary a whisper of air moving today, Pa. It's hot, dry, and we've wasted a whole lot of effort. We'd have sure enough caught sign of them if they had headed for Brown's Ridge or the river."

"Lark and me didn't find squat either," Hyrum told his boys sourly. "Let's hope Sentry and Rojas have had better luck."

"Sentry was an Indian scout for several years," Saul said. "If anyone can find Buster and Butch, it'll be him."

Hyrum glared at Lark. "Your boys sure enough run into trouble. They were supposed to be back day before yesterday."

"The message we got from Millie said Gavin had re-ported back to the office and that he was trailing some bandit up this way," Lark whined in his usual way. "It seemed that splitting up was the best way to find him."

"There's a lot of country up here to look through, and now we've lost your other two sons."

"They might be on Gavin's trail right now," Lark sug-gested. "Maybe they've got him holed up and are closing in on the kill. Millie has never steered us wrong."

"I don't doubt your wife's information," Hyrum said. "But I do say this revenge is a fool's errand. Your son, Jay, was a good boy, one of our own, but he made a mistake going off alone to see his gal. He got himself caught by Gavin and ended up at the end of a rope. We are risking getting caught ourselves by trying to make that law hound pay. All of this hunting and chasing about has taken way too long."

"Me and my boys need this, Hy," Lark whined. "Jay was my eldest, set to take over when I hang up my gun. Butch and Buster both looked up to him."

Hyrum waved a hand. "Yeah, all right. I guess I'm just getting grumpy in my old age. Seems we ought to be pulling a couple of jobs and then spending our money on good times. You know, sitting back with our feet up on a stool, a bottle of snake juice in one hand and a dancehall gal in the other. I'm getting where I hate sleeping on the trail."

"Durn it all, Hy, we knew life would be tough when we started rustling cattle back when the boys were hardly old enough to ride. You know I haven't seen Millie in over three years." He sighed. "She went to the trial and had to watch them sentence Jay to hang. Great thing for a mother to see."

"You've got that right. I'm surprised she even answered your letter."

"Ain't no love lost betwixt us anymore, but she does have that friend who keeps her posted about the doings from the U.S. Marshals' office. They wanted Gavin to go into hiding, but he went after some holdup man called the Gentleman Bandit down this way instead."

"I would guess she's likely more than a little bitter over your boy being hanged."

Lark agreed. "Him being our first, and he being the only one in the family who didn't have the horse-face looks, she tended to show him more favor that the other two."

"Jay was something special, all right." Hyrum chuckled. "I still remember when the boy was about twelve and tossed his loop on that old moss-horned bull. Bet that beast weighed close to a ton."

Lark laughed at the memory. "I spent a whole day following after the three of them—Jay, his horse, and that bull."

"Your boy was smart enough to keep moving," Hyrum pointed out. "Finally run that bull to ground."

"About wind-broke his horse doing it," Lark added. "And then we had to turn the moss-horned critter loose."

"Yonder is some dust." Saul broke into their reminiscing. "It should be Sentry and Rojas." Several minutes passed, and Saul was proven correct. Sentry was a tall man with the beak and eyes of an eagle. His hawklike nose was offset somewhat by his bushy mustache. He had large hands and feet but still moved with agility. Rojas had been his sidekick since the Indian wars, joining up with him when they both finished their hitch with the cavalry. They had done some bounty hunting together and pulled a small job or two before they met up with the Quinteens. At the time, Hyrum had been planning to steal a big company payroll from a train. After joining the gang and with the successful robbery, they had tagged along for another dozen holdups and bank jobs. They had been part of the gang now for almost two years.

"We found their trail," Sentry said, stopping his horse before the eagerly waiting group. "Located a lame horse back in the hills and found tracks leading out of a box canyon. The way I read the signs, it appears Buster and Butch set up an ambush, but something went wrong. Couldn't tell much, except three horses continued on out of the hills. From the direction they took, it looks as if they are headed for Sunset."

"Hard to believe the boys would get the drop on the marshal and then end up going to Sunset," Lark said.

"What do you make of that?" Saul asked.

Lark only shrugged, while Hyrum asked Sentry, "Any idea who the crippled horse belonged to?"

"It wasn't the lawman's. We know he rides a big sorrel, and this was a shaggy old bay. The saddle and some other stuff were left behind where it had been stripped. Didn't have much in them other than a change of clothes for a man about Moab's size." He added, "The outfit was something a dude might wear, a bit on the fancy side and," he finished meaningfully, "a black silk bandanna."

"Some fancy Dan, huh?" Lark said.

"Fancy Dan nothing," Hyrum snorted, deducing the indication. "It's the Gentleman Bandit. That blasted marshal got his man—again!"

"Same as he got Jay," Moab said.

Hyrum gave a nod. "I'd guess the bandit's horse came up lame, and the marshal caught up with him."

Lark surmised, "And somehow the marshal must have gotten the drop on Buster and Butch afterward. That slippery sidewinder ended up with the bandit and my two sons as his prisoners."

"You're sure of the signs?" Hyrum asked. "The boys didn't just follow the tracks of the marshal's horse?"

Sentry shook his head. "There were some boot prints and scuff marks on the ground—a drop or two of blood too—and it reads all three horses left together."

"No reason the boys would go to Sunset if they had captured the marshal," Lark deduced.

"I'm getting real curious about this here deputy," Saul said thickly. "How the hell does a lawman with a prisoner get the best of Buster and Butch?"

"The question piques my interest too," Moab said, joining with his brother. "One marshal against three? I can't figure any way he would end up on top in a pile like that."

"Blast his hide! I want to see him dead!" Lark exploded.

"What's the plan?" Sentry asked Hyrum.

"Regardless of what happens with the Gentleman Bandit, a man would be a fool to try to take Butch and Buster all the way to Denver on his own. So far, this Marshal Gavin don't fit as any fool."

"You think he will stop at Sunset?" Moab wondered.

"They have a telegraph there," Sentry informed the others. "I remember it from back when I rode through there a couple years back."

"Makes sense for him to wire for help," Rojas said, putting in a rare opinion. "No way he would try and move three prisoners over a hundred miles on his own."

Hyrum glanced skyward and then looked at Lark. "It's getting on to sundown. We'll find some water and make camp. Tomorrow we'll head for Sunset and see about finding your boys."

"And maybe get us some payback at the same time," Saul said. "Ain't that right, Pa?"

"The marshal's days are numbered, and the count is growing short," Hyrum agreed. "Let find a spot for the night."

At Latigo's continued insistence, and with the dim possibility of maybe dancing with either Cleo or Dee, Wes arrived at the dance shortly after the music started. Entering the barn, he discovered a table set up with a bowl of punch and some pastries. Beyond the table, numerous bales of straw had been arranged along the walls for people to sit on. The center of the barn was clear, except for a little straw covering the hard-packed dirt floor. As for the band, it consisted of two men with fiddles and a piano player. They had obviously played together before, as they were in unison and featured some lively tunes.

Wes wished Latigo had come along, or even Shep, so he would have some company. Making the best of the situation, he poured himself a glass of punch and picked up a sweet roll. He selected a vacant bale of straw, sat down, and looked over the crowd while he snacked.

As might be expected, the men outnumbered the women about five to one, so his chances of dancing with either of the pretty girls he'd met since arriving were pretty slim. Along with the married couples, he spotted both Cleo and Dee. It didn't appear either of them would be sitting out any dances. He also noticed the three men he had encountered upon his arrival in town, the trio that had been ready to take Glen from the cell through the use of force. They were passing a flask of liquor among them and stayed pretty much to themselves.

The evening wore on, and after asking a question or two of bystanders and listening to small talk, he learned the identities of the three men. Kip Rycott was clearly the leader, about average in size, with Scat Upton easily being the largest man in the room. As for Pepper York, he had unruly black hair, a bit of a hook nose, and was not as big as most of the women. One other fellow pointed out for him was Emmett Dodge, the Van Ness ranch foreman. He was a regular-looking cowboy who danced with Dee Johnson about every other tune. Cleo was more fickle, seldom dancing with the same partner for more than a single song.

As the current melody came to an end, a man waved his hand for attention. The piano player played a loud introductory strain and displayed a wide grin.

"Yes, well, thanks for the support, Sid," the speaker acknowledged good-naturedly. "And it's good to see everyone is having fun tonight."

"We'd have a lot more fun, Mayor, if you'd figure a way to get more women to come to Sunset!" a man called out.

The mayor laughed and retorted, "It's hard to find a woman who will put up with you bunch of no-account yahoos and drifters." The words brought a round of laughter from the crowd before he continued. "But let us not forget the ladies we do have in Sunset. I'd wager there's no finer female stock in the country than we have right here!"

Those words brought a rousing cheer from the men. The mayor lifted his hands to quiet the group once more. "However," he began again, "it's tough for a single lady to get a chance to meet some of the more standoffish gents of our fair community. Therefore, this next dance will be *lady's choice*. The band will play a slow number, so you gals don't get your feet stomped by some cowboy who never learned how to stay in step with the music." He waited out a few shouts and jeers. "We'll take a short break to allow you gals time to talk your choice into taking a turn around the floor." He pulled out his timepiece. "Let's say ten minutes." And with another glance over the crowd, he added, "Good luck to everyone."

Wes was smiling about the mayor's presentation when a shadow fell over him. He looked up as a second shadow arrived. To his shock, both Cleo and Dee were standing in front of him!

"What's the idea, *Cleopatra*?" Dee purposely drawled the name, challenging the Van Ness girl in a haughty tone of voice. "This guy has your brother in his jail."

"It's not *his* jail, and he's not holding my brother, *Delight*," she shot back, her own voice oozing the name with equal disdain. "He has two prisoners of his own." She squared off to face Dee. "Besides, what do you want with him?"

"He gave me a story," Dee fired back. "What did he give you?"

"A sizable bruise," she retorted with some force, "in a place I won't be showing you or anyone else!"

"I know what you're up to, Cleopatra," Dee said, poking the other girl in the breastbone with an extended finger. "You're chasing after him to win him over to your side concerning Glen."

Cleo batted the hand away. "And what are you after, Delight—another story? Another article saying that my brother should hang?"

"I watched him kill a man in cold blood. He deserves to hang!"

"You don't know the whole story!" Cleo cried.

"So tell me!" Dee shrieked right back. "I'd love to know what excuse there is for shooting an unarmed man!"

Things were escalating to the boiling point. Wes stood up to intervene. "Ladies, I don't think—"

"You stay out of this!" Dee snapped, cutting his sentence short.

"Yes," said Cleo, ganging up on him too. "No one asked for your opinion!"

"Look, I'm only trying to—"

"Who cares what you were trying to do!" Dee shouted. "This is between Cleopatra and me!"

"Don't be yelling at him!" Cleo shot back. "And stop calling me Cleopatra, *Delight* Johnson!"

Wes sighed and sat back down.

Dee's voice rose an octave. "I should let you take him. It would show everyone in the valley how desperate you are to find a man!"

"You pompous little twerp!" Cleo screamed back. "I suppose you think you took Emmett away from me!"

"Not for a second," Dee retorted. "I'm certain he *ran* away from you—and your whole family!"

The argument was quickly spiraling into a major confrontation. Before the two started slapping or hair-pulling, Wes decided to exercise a sensible option, the opposite of valor. He got to his feet and physically pushed between them.

"If you'll excuse me, *ladies*," he said sarcastically. "I'm going over to the jail to relieve Latigo. I believe there's less chance of my getting killed guarding a roomful of murderers."

The smoldering glare from each girl warned him not to look back over his shoulder. He strode smartly out of the barn and didn't stop until he reached the jail.

"Lat . . . Shep?" he called out. "I'm coming in."

"Come ahead," Latigo replied.

He entered the room and closed the door. Shep was sitting behind the desk, while Latigo was resting his haunches on the corner of the desktop.

"So how'd it go?" Latigo asked at once.

"I'm going to catch a little shut-eye and will be back to relieve you boys around midnight."

"It went that bad?" Shep wanted to know.

"If I told you, you wouldn't believe me—and that's the truth."

Chapter Six

Cleo rode in the buckboard with Raul Gomez, one of the old wranglers from the ranch, who had driven her into town. He was retired from most of the physical work at the ranch, but he still lived there. Instead of doing much out on the range, he puttered around with odd jobs and was often handy to saddle a horse or hitch up a buggy for one of the family. He was a man of few words who did a lot of hunting and fishing between chores.

Emmett came riding up from behind, catching them at about the halfway point to the ranch. He had Gomez trade places with him and take his horse on to the ranch. Once beside Cleo, he started the buggy moving again.

"All right," Cleo said, after a few moments of silence, "what's on your mind, Emmett?"

"Kip, Scat, and Pepper are still in town," he informed her. "I think they might cause trouble before this thing with Glen is over."

Cleo gritted her teeth. "Father warned them to stay out of this."

"They get a few drinks under their belts, and they're not going to remember his advice."

She muttered an oath. "It was stupid the way they tried to go against Shep and take Glen out of jail. What's the matter with them? Don't they know Glen has to face this, do the prison time if necessary, and put it behind him?"

Emmett grunted. "I'm sometimes surprised those three think to put their hats on when it rains."

"I'll speak to Daddy," she promised. "You don't think they would try anything tonight?"

"That deputy U.S. marshal and his pal are still in town. With three of them watching the jail, I don't see how they could expect to get Glen out. At least, not without getting some people killed."

They rode in silence for a few minutes, before Emmett asked, "So what was the scrap between you and Dee tonight?" He turned so he could look at Cleo. "I went out for a smoke, and when I came back, it looked as if you and her were going to claw each other's eyes out."

"It was nothing."

"Someone said you were fighting over the new tin star."

She threw him a hard look. "We weren't fighting over a man!"

"Lady's choice dance . . . you and she standing in front of the same guy?" He shrugged. "Can't blame me for being curious."

"Are you afraid Delight might have eyes for another man? Is that what you're worried about?"

"Dee says she's very fond of me, but she has not made me any promises."

"At least her father isn't an obstacle," she said, thinking back to when Emmett had attempted to court her.

"No, Dee isn't worried about what her father will think, being that she's twenty-one and has a mind of her own."

"She's headstrong and independent, I'll grant you that."

"This story of Glen shooting that drifter is the first time she's been able to write anything of real importance. Everything up to now has been unexciting news about a new baby or a wedding. This is the kind of reporting she's always wanted to do."

"Dee never lacked for ambition," Cleo said. Then, with a sympathetic look at Emmett, she added, "I'm not sure how good a wife she'll make."

The ranch foreman chose not to pursue the subject. "What do you think we ought to do about Kip and the others? Those three simpleminded sots might try to break Glen out."

"They hadn't better, not with Deputy Marshal Gavin on the job. He's not a store clerk like Shep; I saw him draw his gun. He would cut them down like weeds in a garden."

"You saw him draw his gun?" he asked incredulously.

She waved a hand to dismiss his concern. "It was nothing. I surprised him when I walked into the jail."

"Hot dang! If your pa heard the guy had turned a gun on you . . ."

"He's not going to hear about it!" she said decisively, rotating to pin Emmett with an icy gaze. "I told you that in strict confidence."

"All right," he acquiesced at once. "I won't say anything."

"You'd better not. It was my fault for barging into the jail without knocking first. He was watching three prisoners and had already butted heads with Kip and his pals when they tried to take Glen away from Shep. Plus Uncle Fremont told me the two killers that the marshal brought in were part of a gang who might try to break them out. The man was bound to be a little edgy."

Emmett decided to get back to his original line of questions. "I'm still surprised Ogden is willing to let Glen stand trial for murder. Did Glen tell you anything that might help his case?"

"Glen said the dead man and his pal cheated him at cards the last time he was in town. That's about all."

"But he did say the man pulled a gun?"

Cleo gave a nod of her head. "Yes. He said he had warned the guy not to come back after losing his money to him the last time. He didn't intend to kill the man. He tossed him out of the saloon and was going to run him out of town. Then the guy pulled a gun, and he had to shoot."

"And your pa thinks using that story as a defense, without having a gun to prove it, will save Glen from a noose?"

"I don't know, Emmett!" She was irked at his insistence. "Shep didn't find the gun, so the gambler's partner must have taken it."

"How about Dee? She didn't want to talk about it to me. Did she see the guy reach for a gun or not? Is that what you two were fighting about?"

"We were not fighting," she corrected him. "It was a . . . disagreement, and it was over her trying to get Glen hanged. She knows nothing about the gambler's cheating or anything of his pal. All she saw was Glen shoot the man."

"She was the one closest to the shooting," Emmett pointed out. "She is going to be the main witness against him." He heaved a sigh. "Dee can be very convincing."

"Yes. Yes, she can," she said, unable to hide the dread she felt.

Emmett returned to watching the trail ahead. "Well, the only thing I know is, those three hands are going to cause trouble before this is over. They wouldn't listen to me."

"What are you doing chasing after them instead of seeing Delight home?"

"*Dee*"—he accented the name the girl preferred— "went home with her father." He grunted. "First time I ever knew her to prefer his company over mine."

"I believe she was hoping to get another story out of the marshal."

"And what were you hoping to get out of him?"

"A dance, is all," she said, perhaps too quickly. "I want him to be supportive of Glen's situation."

"Your brother isn't his prisoner. Why should it matter one way or the other to him?"

"He's a lawman of some importance. If he believes Glen's side of the shooting, it might go a long way with a judge."

"Silly me, I thought maybe you felt a spark for him."

"He's just another stranger passing through town, that's all."

"Yeah, I suppose you're right. Besides which, Deputy Marshal Gavin ain't all that special." Emmett spoke matter-of-factly, but Cleo missed the warning sign. "I doubt most women would call him handsome, but I guess a few might find him slightly less repulsive than discovering a garden spider in their soup."

"He does have a pleasing smile and gentle eyes," Cleo responded automatically, picturing the man in her head. "I mean"—she recovered from the unwitting remark at once—"for a man of his profession."

"I noticed that too," Emmett teased. "Even from across the barn, I couldn't help but notice his gentle eyes."

Cleo punched him in the ribs.

"Yee-ouch!" Emmett exclaimed. "I didn't know you liked him that much."

"I don't know him well enough to like him *that much*, Emmett. And don't you be saying anything to the contrary to Father."

"Mum's the word," he said, rubbing his ribs. "You can trust me, Cleo. I like breathing too much to say anything."

Wes awoke a little before midnight. He strapped on his gun, put on his hat and boots, and then exited his room. He stretched mightily and began the walk over to relieve Latigo and Shep. He had only gone a few steps when he heard somebody whispering. Keeping to the shadows, he eased around the edge of the tanner's shop to see what was going on in the alleyway. There was a two-by-one-foot opening near the roof of the stout-built jail, allowing for both air circulation and light, but the height of the window and the narrowness of the opening prevented any idea of escape. With only a single lamp inside the marshal's office, turned low for the night, there was barely a glimmer of light from the portal to illuminate the passageway.

He could make out three men in the darkness and drew his gun, ready to shoot instantly. If these were part of the Quinteen gang, it was going to be a kill-or-be-killed gunfight.

"Thar it be," the largest of the three whispered, his words slurred from too much drink. "Bet that"—he belched—"bet that's the winder we're lookin' for."

"Quiet, Scat!" one of the others said. "You want to have that there marshal down on our backs?"

"Him and his badge don't worry me none, Kip," the third one, a man of small stature, laughed. "He climbs my hump, I'll shore 'nuff give him a toss! Yes, sir, just like a green mustang!"

"Bejesus! You guys are both logged to the gills with scamper juice!" Kip complained. "I'd have been better off coming alone."

Wes recognized the three men he had encountered upon his arrival in town, the same three he had seen drinking at the dance. They were obviously up to mischief.

"I need a boost, Pepper," Scat ordered. "I'm taller than either of you, but I still can't reach that winder. You act like a step-up, and I'll pass a gun through the bars." He chuckled. "Glen will get the drop on Shep, and he's a free man!"

It was a moment when Wes could have stepped out of

the shadows and taken charge of the situation. But the little guy called Pepper immediately dropped to his hands and knees and then crawled over next to the building. Wes watched the absurdity unfold as Scat placed a foot up onto his back. The problem with their scheme was that Scat probably weighed about the same as a fair-sized steer. Pepper might have weighed a hundred pounds if he first filled his pockets with rocks. When Scat put his weight on his foot, Pepper flattened right out on the ground with a groan. Paying him no mind, the bigger man didn't stop from stepping aboard with his second foot.

"You guys are both knot-heads!" Kip lamented. "Pepper can't hold you up high enough to do any good, Scat!"

The big black man stuck up his arm, still a few inches shy of reaching the opening. "I can almost reach, Kip," he said. "If you was to lay on top of Pepper, I betcha I could reach the winder."

"This ain't gonna work," Pepper gasped, unable to breathe with the bigger man standing on his back. "I'm dying here!"

"Get off him, you big oaf!" Kip growled. He took hold of Scat's belt and gave a hard yank. With his uncertain footing and being so drunk, he could hardly stand, and Scat went easily in the direction of the pull—too easily. He rotated around as he felt himself falling and caught hold of Kip's shoulders. Kip wasn't much more sober than his buddies. He collapsed under the weight of the large man.

The three of them ended up in a tangle of arms and

legs, sprawled about on the ground together, all swearing and trying to figure out which direction was up. Wes waded in and quickly removed their pistols from their holsters. By the time they managed sitting positions, he had them disarmed and under his gun.

"It's a stinkin' trap!" Scat bemoaned. "The law was waiting for us."

"You two made a hell of a mess of this," Kip wailed. "Now we're in a tar pit right up to our lower lips!"

Wes looked over the three inept clowns, swallowed the mirth that threatened to surface, and managed a stern voice. "You boys are in big trouble. Trying to break a man out of jail is a serious crime. I suspect you will all be busting rock at the nearest prison for the next ten years. What do you have to say for yourselves?"

Kip's shoulders sagged in defeat. "It wasn't much of a plan. We got to drinking and . . . well, we were only looking to get our pal out of jail."

"That window you were trying to reach is not Glen's cell; it's the one for the Quinteen boys. Give them a gun, and they would likely kill Glen and all three of you during their bust-out. They aren't the sort to leave witnesses."

Scat's head rolled on his shoulders as if he was utterly perplexed. "It didn't sound like such a bad idea when we was drinkin'. But I can see now how it weren't the smartest thing we could do."

"And you, Pepper?" Wes asked, looking at the third man. "What do you say?"

"I think Scat broke my back." Pepper grimaced, trying to rub himself where the man's heavy boots had left their marks. "Man weighs twice as much drunk as he does sober."

"What's going on out here?" Latigo's voice came out of the darkness. He had heard the commotion and come to investigate.

"It's nothing to worry about now," Wes said back to him. "These three geniuses thought they would pass a gun through the window to their pal."

The old gent had a shotgun in his hands. He walked over to stand next to Wes and cocked back the hammers. "Ain't no more room in the jail, Marshal, and that's the gospel truth." He set himself and took aim. "You want that I should shoot them?"

Wes gave a slow shake of his head, as if there was no alternative. "It's about the only thing we can do."

Kip's eyes widened, his mouth opened, and he threw up his hands. "Now, hold on!" he cried. "You can't just shoot us!"

"Hello, Saint Peter!" Pepper wailed, hastily crossing himself. "I'm on my way."

"Hey, no!" Scat's expression was sheer panic. He scooted away until his back was against the wall of the jail. "We didn't mean no one any harm."

Wes rested a hand on the barrel of the shotgun, as if to prevent Latigo from firing the gun. He kept a hard edge to his voice. "Look at it from our side, boys. We can't put you in a cell because we've got a full house. And if I turn you loose, you'll be back here tomorrow or the next day trying something like this again. Latigo is right. The only option I have is to let him shoot you here and now."

"There's other options!" Kip piped up anxiously.

"Yeah. What he said," Pepper agreed at once.

Scat jumped in with his partners. "I don't know what that *option* thing is, but I'm for it too."

"Don't listen to their whining, Marshal." Latigo remained austere. "Better to let me shoot them and be done with it."

"That scattergun would wake up the whole town," Wes said. "Hate to roust people out of their sleep over this."

"You don't gotta shoot us at all!" Kip wailed. "We'll be good. We promise!"

Wes fixed his gaze on Kip. "I suppose you three would give me your word of honor that you wouldn't try something again?"

"Yeah! Hell, yeah!" Kip exclaimed.

Pepper added his own, "You can trust us!"

As for the big man, his head was bobbing up and down about as jerkily as a ball rolling down a flight of stairs.

Wes remained undecided. "I've no one to vouch for you boys. I'd like to take your word, but how do I know you are honorable sorts?"

"Ask the barkeep at the Red Rose," Scat volunteered. "He knows us."

Pepper joined in again. "Sure enough. We've never run up a bill and not paid it in full. And we ain't never had no trouble in his place neither, less'n you count a harmless fight or two."

"Isn't that place owned by one of Glen Van Ness' relatives?"

Kip had sobered quickly. "No, sir. That's the Silver Dollar Casino. The man who owns the Red Rose ain't even a close friend of Ogden or Glen."

"Though he does have something of a torch burning for Miss Cleo," Scat offered.

Both Kip and Pepper paused from worrying about saving their hides long enough to throw a hard look at the big man, telling him to keep quiet.

"I don't know," Wes said thoughtfully. "This here is a pretty serious crime."

Latigo did not budge. "I still say you ought to let me shoot them. Probably be doing the country a favor. What if one of them was to have offspring one day?"

"That's a valid point, Lat."

"Us? Have offspring?" Kip uttered a contemptuous laugh. "What woman in her right mind would marry one of us?"

"Yeah," Pepper sounded off, "ain't a gal in the country who would be caught dead with me or Kip. And Scat has always said he never wants to get hitched."

"That's the truth," Scat declared. "I ain't the kind of guy to settle down with a wife and kids. I like running free and wild with Kip and Pepper."

"See?" Kip said. "We aren't about to have families. You can trust us to stay shed of marriage for the rest of our lives."

Wes looked at the Gentleman Bandit. "The boys make a strong argument. Who would ever marry one of them?"

Kip saw there might be a glimmer of hope and pressed the advantage. "You let us go, and we'll do right by you, Marshal," he promised. "More'n that, if you get into any trouble, you only have to give a holler, and we'll come running to help."

"What kind of trouble do I have to worry about?"

"We know about them fellows you brung to jail. I've heard about the Quinteen gang." Kip was talking fast. "What do those two inside the cell have, maybe a half dozen cousins? And then there's a father and uncles and friends too. We heard you had wired for a prison wagon because you don't dare travel with them alone."

"So you're offering to help?"

Kip raised a hand as if to swear an oath. "You let us go, and if the Quinteen gang comes looking for trouble, you can count on us three to stand with you against them."

"That's a mighty brave offer," Latigo said, voicing his own opinion. "For myself, I was thinking of hiding under the porch until the shooting was over."

Wes holstered his gun. "All right, you three. Here's the deal. You promise not to try to bust Glen out of jail again, and to lend a hand if the Quinteen gang rides into town. You give me your word on those two things, and you're free to ride out."

Never had Wes been so overwhelmed with vows, oaths, and promises. The three men about knocked him down rushing over to shake his hand and pound him on the back. Then they retrieved their guns and headed off into the night to get their horses.

Latigo was still at his side when the three men rode past. They all waved and called good night—softly, of course, so they wouldn't wake up the town. When the riders were out of sight, Latigo laughed. "Think they'll sober up and remember offering to fight against the Quinteen gang?"

"I don't know, Lat. I only hope they remember the part about not trying to break Glen out of jail again."

Chapter Seven

Ogden was on the front porch of the house. It was Sunday morning, so Emmett and Raul were harnessing a team to the four-passenger buggy for the family trip into town for worship. Cleo walked outside to stand next to Ogden, while her mother was finishing getting ready.

Kip and his two pals were up and moving, though all of them looked to have major hangovers. As they passed the porch, the trio said good morning.

"I'm glad to see you boys are all here today," Cleo said to stop them. "I was afraid you might do something stupid last night after the dance."

Ogden took a stride in their direction and regarded them with a warning scowl. "You men aren't still thinking about breaking Glen out of jail? I thought I made it clear that my son is to stand trial."

"Us? Try and bust him out?" Kip mirrored complete innocence. "Not on your life, Mr. Van Ness."

Scat rolled his eyes at the thought. "The three of us

have done sworn not to do anything that might be breaking the law in Sunset."

"Or risk hurting Shep or Marshal Gavin," Kip avowed.

Ogden was not convinced. "You tried to take Glen out
once by force. I heard a rumor you boys stayed in town
last night and were of a mind to try again, deputy marshal in town or not."

Kip gave a negative shake of his head and appeared
taken aback at the idea. "No, sir!" he declared. "Marshal
Gavin is about the most decent and honorable man we
ever met. We got nothing but respect for him."

"That's right," Scat agreed. "Anyone messes with that
there marshal has got to deal with us."

Cleo gaped in awe as she stepped up even with Ogden.
She forcibly shut her mouth and exchanged a baffled look
with her father. At his shrug, she put her attention on Pepper. He seemed to be walking as stiffly as a crippled man
on stilts. "How about you, Pepper?" she asked. "Do you
feel the same way?"

"I only feel a powerful ache in my back," he whined.
"I think I must have gotten run over by a runaway
freight wagon last night."

Emmett climbed into the buggy and turned it around
for the drive to town. Raul wandered off, his work finished for the day, as Emmett pulled the carriage over to
the porch. The ranch foreman stared after the three men
as they continued on their way toward the bunkhouse.

"What do you think about that?" he asked Ogden and
Cleo.

"I don't believe it!" Cleo exclaimed. "Marshal Gavin

is the *most decent and honorable* man they ever met? They've nothing but respect for him? And they are willing to take his side in a fight? What on earth is going on?"

"It's a puzzle to me as well," Ogden admitted.

"What's a puzzle?" Naomi asked, having come out of the house to overhear the end of their conversation.

"Nothing, Mother," Cleo responded. "Only I'm beginning to think Marshal Gavin should run for governor. It seems everyone is on his side about everything."

Emmett, still seated and holding the reins to the team, looked after the hired hands and remarked, "Pepper is moving like his horse sat on him. I wonder what did happen last night."

"It's a mystery to us all," Ogden answered.

"I don't know what you three are talking about, but we'd better get a move on," Naomi said. "We don't want to be late to the meeting."

Wes had finished another breakfast of mush and stale bread. It seemed he ate no better than his prisoners lately. Once he was relieved by Shep and Latigo, he left the jail and started for his room behind the tanner shop. He didn't get far before he was accosted by Dee Johnson. She arrived panting from her short run to intercept him. The physical effort caused a lock of her dark hair to come loose on one side from the swirling bun at the back of her head. She brushed at the pesky strand, eyes bright and dancing with excitement, as she blocked his path.

"Mr. Dykes said you stopped a jailbreak last night." She gasped the words.

"What were you doing talking to Latigo?"

"A good reporter never sleeps. I saw him over at Bertha's, getting breakfast for you and the prisoners. Is it true about some men trying to break Glen out of jail?"

"It was nothing. A couple guys drank more than they could handle. There was little chance they would have broken anyone out of jail."

"I'm impressed by how modest you are," she praised him. "Most men crow like roosters whenever they do anything worthy of note."

"As I said, Miss Johnson, it was nothing of consequence."

"I suppose the day you arrived and saved Shep from possibly being killed, that was of no consequence either."

"Those men didn't want to hurt anyone. They were pushing to see if Shep would back down. I doubt any gunplay would have ever come about."

Dee lowered her notepad and gazed directly at him. Wes read the intensity in her, as if she had a thousand questions to ask. When she spoke, however, he was startled by the subject matter.

"I'm sorry we didn't get our dance," she said with the utmost sincerity.

"Uh, me too," he managed awkwardly.

"Perhaps we could go for a walk together after the church meeting."

"I spent most of the night at the jail guarding the prisoners. I don't think I'd be great company. In fact, I was on my way over to my room to catch a few hours of sleep."

A tight little frown came to her face. "Are you purposely avoiding me? Am I such an ogre that you don't wish to be seen with me?"

"Hell—" He caught himself at once. "I mean, shucks, no. You're about the prettiest gal I ever set eyes on. And being smart isn't a sin in my book either."

"So why haven't you tried to pursue me? Why am I the one doing the pursuing?"

"I figure you're only looking for another story, what with you being an avid reporter for the newspaper. Most gals aren't interested in getting to know a man who is just passing through their town. They don't see any future in it."

"I'm not desperately searching for a husband, if that's what you are inferring. I'm in no hurry to get married and have kids. I want to be a reporter, but I also enjoy spending time and having a conversation with an intelligent man."

"I spend weeks or months chasing after wanted outlaws, and then I spend my days watching over them like a prison guard. I don't reckon my idea of intelligence is quite the same as yours."

A wagon approached from up the street and stopped next to numerous others at the barn, the only place in town big enough for a Sunday meeting. Wes was facing the wrong way to see the new arrival without completely turning around, but he spied an impish sort of gleam within the girl's eyes.

"Let's agree to get together sometime. Okay?" Dee suggested. Before Wes could manage a reply, she came up onto her toes and kissed him on the cheek. She pulled back at once and offered him a dazzling smile.

"That's for giving me updates for the newspaper. You're very sweet."

Wes stood dumbly as Dee swirled her skirt and minced away, seeming about as merry as a mischievous forest sprite. It took only a glance over at the buggy that had just arrived to understand why. Cleo and Emmett were on the front bench, along with an elderly couple seated on the rear cushions. All four had apparently witnessed Dee's act of endearment. Emmett glowered at him, while Cleo glared after Dee with a contemptuous, hawklike scrutiny.

"Starving dogs all around," Wes muttered to himself, "and me the single bone they've chosen to fight over." With a groan, he asked, "Don't I have enough to worry about?"

Latigo chuckled, having been watching from the jail window when Dee first rushed over to Wes. He mentioned what he had seen to Shep, and the young man laughed.

"Those two gals have been one-upping each other for as long as I can remember. Both of them are smart and pretty, and the competition between them has been a part of Sunset's makeup for years. Makes no difference if it's baked goods being judged at the fall festival or trying to best one another in a footrace. A couple years ago, they both spent a small fortune on dresses from back east, each trying to outdo the other for the Christmas dance."

"Who usually wins?" Latigo asked.

"I don't keep score, and I don't think they do either. But you can bet your hat that if one of them shows an interest in something, so does the other." Shep came to the window and pointed at the wagon. "See the young guy, the one who drove the team?" At a nod from Latigo, he told him, "That's Emmett Dodge, the foreman of the Van Ness ranch. He was on Cleo's arm for a short while, and now he is on Dee's leash."

"So now them two gals have both decided to have a go at the marshal," Latigo deduced.

Shep continued to grin. "He'll be lucky to get out of town in one piece—and that's not counting the Quinteen boys or their gang."

Latigo took a seat at the desk, while Shep continued to stand at the window. He liked the young man. He had courage and a sense of honor and was an upstanding member of the community.

"Where do you hail from, Shep?"

"Been in Colorado my whole life. Ma raised me by herself after my father deserted us."

"That so?"

Shep shrugged. "She told me he left because we were penniless and sleeping in an abandoned shed. I was too young to remember much, maybe six or seven at the time, and I guess times were hard. My mother told me how my father had not been able to find work, and we were about to starve. He finally stole some money to buy food for us, and the sheriff came looking. That's the last time I saw my father."

"What did your mother do?"

"We were taken in by another family for a short time, but then some money arrived by stage, and we were able to get a place of our own. It was only a shack, but to us, it was a mansion." He grew pensive for a time but continued with his history. "Mom took in laundry and cleaned houses or tended children for folks. Every few weeks another envelope would arrive with some money in it. I didn't know until I was half-grown that the money was from my father."

"Then he didn't desert you completely," Latigo said.

"Mom never said much about him, but I think she figured he was not coming by the money honestly. She took the money and used it for us, but I know it was only because she had me to raise. Had she been alone in the world, I'm certain she would never have touched a dime."

"You had a rough go growing up," Latigo said.

Shep shrugged his shoulders. "I took to working as soon as anyone would hire me and began to earn our keep. A year or so after my ma died, the money finally stopped. Knowing it was dishonest money, I gave the last delivery to the parson to help other folks in need. I guess I was near twenty when the payments stopped."

"Sounds like your mother taught you a real sense of right and wrong."

"Yep, she didn't allow for me to stray far from the straight-and-narrow growing up."

"And you never wondered about your father?"

Shep grimaced. "Sure, I wondered why he deserted us. I mean, everyone has tough times in their life. It's no excuse for going out and robbing or stealing from someone else. I can't help but think he could have found another way to see we didn't starve."

"You're a good, honest man, Shep," Latigo told him with complete sincerity. "I'll bet your father would be right proud to call you his son."

"Yeah? Well, I wish I could say the same for him."

Latigo felt an ache deep inside and let the subject drop. "I'll keep an eye on our guests today. You ought to spend Sunday with your wife and kids."

"I hate for you to do my job for me."

He snorted at the notion. "The Quinteen boys are me and the marshal's responsibility. Besides, I've nowhere to go and nothing else to do. You go ahead. I'll be fine until Wes comes back."

"I'll take you up on the offer. But I will see that dinner is sent over for you and the prisoners," Shep promised.

"That would be fine. See you later."

Shep left the office, and Latigo followed him with his gaze. What a fine young man his son had become. Too bad he had a father who was going to spend the rest of his life behind bars. He would have enjoyed being a grand-father and, maybe one day, trying to make things right between him and Shep.

"There she be," Lark Quinteen said, stopping his horse at the crest of the hill. "Sunset."

"Fair size for a town this far off the beaten trail," Moab said. "I expected a small settlement or a few houses and a trading post."

Sentry was at his side. "This place is a crossroad to Wyoming, Utah, and New Mexico, so it gets a lot of trav-elers, pilgrims, miners, drovers, and such. I remember it had two saloons and several stores."

"We gonna ride right in and take a look?" Saul asked.

"Could be that Buster and Butch are sitting in a cell waiting for us," Moab chimed in.

Hyrum held up a hand to stop the chatter. "We don't ride in until we know what we're up against. Sentry is the man who has ridden this way before." He rotated in the saddle and looked at him. "Does the town have a lawman and a jail?"

"I recollect they didn't have a full-time sheriff, only some guy who filled in when needed. But there's a jail, and it was sturdy looking." He grinned. "I tend to notice whenever a town has a jail."

"There's quite a family resemblance between the boys and the rest of us. Rather than risk our being recognized, you and Rojas will have to do the looking around."

Sentry grew thoughtful. "I've an idea as to how to go about this without drawing too much interest. Rojas and I started out as bounty hunters. We can ride into town like we're looking for the Quinteen gang. With there being a fair price on you and the others, that will explain our purpose in asking questions."

Hyrum chuckled. "Good thinking. No one would suspect you to be asking questions about us and yourselves."

"Think they might be holding Buster and Butch in jail there, Pa?" Moab asked.

"I don't know. But the marshal will have to hole up somewhere while he gets some help from Denver. Once we find the boys, we'll figure a plan to get them back."

Sentry said, "Being Sunday, most folks will be doing a church meeting or family stuff. But we can visit the saloons and pick up the information we need. Shouldn't take but a couple hours."

"You'll find us down at the crossing, where we stopped

to water the horses a few minutes back. We'll fix something to eat, so you two grab a bite while you're snooping around."

"Sounds good. We can find out what's going on and meet back later this afternoon."

Hyrum grunted his approval. "If Lark's boys ain't in the jail, find out which way they went, so we can get on their trail."

"Will do," Sentry promised. Then he and Rojas started down the hill, angling to where they would pick up the main trail leading into town.

"I hope Buster and Butch are there," Moab said. "If that marshal headed for Denver, he could be a full day ahead of us."

"Man would be a fool to try and travel alone with my boys," Lark said.

"Unless he got some help," Hyrum warned. "He might have hired a man or two right here in Sunset to help guard his prisoners."

They sat and watched until their two riders entered town. Then Hyrum led the way back down to the trail in the direction of the creek crossing. The sun was high overhead, so they should know something while they still had a few hours of daylight. For Hyrum, this little chore could not pass quickly enough. Lark's boys never had been the cream on a container of milk, more like the tiny bits of grit that settled to the bottom. His own boys, Moab and Saul, were much quicker of mind and knew how to follow orders.

Lark himself was basically weak and had never used

the back of his hand to instill respect or obedience with his three sons. His wife was too good for him, but it took her three boys and fifteen years to figure that out. She never tried to get a divorce, as that was both a lengthy and costly process. Instead, she had simply given up on Lark and their sons, moving in with her sister and finding work to support herself in Denver. Lark had taken the boys and come to live with Hyrum and his sons. A widower himself, he and his two sons ran an old ranch with a few head of cattle—usually stolen and held just long enough to sell off. For a time, the boys stayed at the house while he and Lark pulled small jobs or rustled cattle with their cousin Mort Franklin. They earned enough to get by until the boys were old enough to start riding with them. With more guns, the jobs grew from petty stealing or robbery to rustling fifty or more head of cattle at a time. When the bank jobs started to pan out, the rewards for their larceny increased, and they often enjoyed many weeks of drinking, gambling, and partying between jobs. Ten years of living on the move had seasoned the boys into men, and they were now able to shoulder their own weight. It had been good, right up until Jay had gotten himself caught and hanged. Now the other two boys were in custody. They were definitely on a cold streak.

Hyrum anchored his teeth, thinking about it. If not for Lark joining with him, he and his boys would have been less careless with their spending. Fewer jobs would have meant less chance of getting caught. Instead, all of them were risking their hides to save Lark's worthless sons.

His brother had always been weak, dependent upon Hyrum for guidance and even his survival. When it came to family, he added greatly to the burden, while giving almost nothing in return. Sometimes it was a real pain to put up with relatives.

Chapter Eight

After the Sunday meeting, Naomi stood with some other wives and caught up on the local gossip. As for Cleo and her father, they went to the jail for a visit with Glen. Latigo allowed they were welcome to speak to the boy. However, when Ogden stepped over to the cell, the temporary deputy motioned for Cleo to come over to the desk.

"Something here you might be interested in," Latigo said. "Deputy Marshal Gavin did the looking and find- ing."

"What are you talking about?" she asked.

"This here dodger." He held up an official-looking handbill. "It might be of interest to you."

Cleo hated that she wasn't a better reader. She slowly pondered the words, discovering the printing to be about two men who were wanted by the law. The notice stated that the pair were gamblers and had staged several crooked card games. One did the playing, while the other would sneak peeks and signal what those at the table were holding in their hands. At other times, they sat in the same game, pretending not to know each other, and would pass their partner cards for the winning hand.

"I'm not sure, what exactly does this mean?" Cleo asked.

"The dodger says the one man was Vic Harmon, who also called himself Duke. The description says he usually wore a fancy embroidered vest and bowler hat." He did not miss her gasp of understanding. "He's wanted for shooting and wounding a man in Pueblo, Colorado," Latigo continued. "From what Dee Johnson told me, the gambler your brother shot was wearing a fancy embroidered vest and one of those bowler hats. He also had a partner."

Cleo felt a rush of anticipation about the paper she held in her hand. "Glen!" she called out, interrupting her father and brother's conversation. "What did you say the dead gambler's name was?"

"He didn't give a real name—went by the handle of Duke. He called his pal Yancy. Never did hear anyone call them by their full names."

"They're outlaws!" she cried. "This is a wanted handbill for their arrest!"

The news brought Ogden hurrying over to the desk. "Outlaws, you say?" He immediately took the dodger and read it over.

Latigo hurried to clarify the situation. "Not much of a crime to cheat at cards, other than occasionally getting your nose busted by an unhappy loser. But that Duke character shot a local banker over in Pueblo and cost him the use of his arm. I believe these two would have served some time behind bars for that, at least the Duke fellow."

"We need to find the partner," Cleo deduced at once.

"You think this could clear my son?" Ogden asked Latigo.

Latigo gave an affirmative bob of his head. "Marshal Gavin said the fact that Duke had shot someone proved he sometimes carried a gun. And the newspaper gal said she saw his pal lean over him to check and see if he was dead. He could have pocketed a hideaway gun before Shep arrived to look over the body."

"Then he left town before anyone could locate him," Cleo said, finishing the story.

"Gavin was going to speak to you or your father about it," Latigo told them.

"Of course, he was"—her voice turned harsh—"except he was too busy cozying up to Delight Johnson and being kissed to remember!"

"Now, Cleo, dear," Ogden said in a calm voice, though he winked at Latigo. "It was only a peck on the cheek. It looked innocent enough to me."

Latigo didn't laugh, but the semblance of a smile wormed its way onto his lips.

"It isn't funny!" Cleo snapped, scowling at both men. "And it wasn't innocent! I know Delight isn't interested in Marshal Gavin; she only wants a story to print."

Latigo lifted a hand to sooth her ire. "Wes is a fairly smart gent. I reckon he knows which of you is genuine and which is counterfeit."

"What is that supposed to mean?" Ogden asked, flashing a curious look at his daughter.

Cleo lifted her eyebrows as if perplexed by the comment. "I don't know what he means, Daddy. I've only spoken to the marshal one time, other than a passing remark at the dance last night. I'm certainly not jealous of Delight Johnson!"

"I should think not," Ogden said a bit smugly.

"No, of course you aren't," Latigo said in agreement. "But the point is, Marshal Gavin spent several hours going through all these old wanted notices just to help your family find a way to prove Glen's innocence. I suspect it's partly because he doesn't like the idea of seeing an innocent man go to jail." She visibly relaxed her defenses. "But," Latigo continued, "I'm right certain he also did some of that research because of what it means to you, Miss Van Ness."

Cleo lowered her eyes to hide an immediate rush of emotion. She took the paper back from her father and studied it, while trying to cope with the insufferable heat that infused her cheeks.

"It says that Yancy character is average height and weight, has a V-shaped scar on his left cheek, and is left-handed," she stated. "Plus he sometimes goes by the full name of Yancy Pine."

Ogden clapped his hands hopefully and returned to Glen to explain what they had learned. As for Cleo, she handed the notice back to Latigo with a hopeful mien.

"Please tell me this will help my brother."

"The fact that Duke had carried a gun is something. But without this guy Yancy in custody, we don't have any real proof there was a gun," Latigo explained. "But there's a chance I might be able to help."

"You? How could you help?"

"I know every hideout or lawless town this side of the Kansas border. There are abandoned mining camps, ghost towns, secluded ranches and farms—a thousand places a man like Yancy could hide—and I know them all."

"Can you do that?" she wanted to know. "Would you help us find him?"

"That's where this problem gets a little complicated." At her puzzled look, he elaborated. "You remember what I told you, about being a prisoner?"

"I thought you were joking."

"No, Marshal Gavin arrested me shortly before we ran into the Quinteen boys. I've given him my word that I won't try to escape, so he has let me help guard these prisoners."

Cleo did not hide her amazement. "He trusts you to keep your word to the point of letting you carry around a gun? I . . . That's incredible."

"I would die before I'd go back on my word to Marshal Gavin," he avowed.

"You said it was complicated?"

"The marshal will have to give me permission to help you find this man. Like I said, I'm the best man for the job, but I would need someone to ride with me. I know where to look, but I don't know the first thing about arresting or transporting a prisoner."

"Emmett could go with you," she said, quickly

volunteering the ranch foreman. "He's very capable, and I would trust him with my life."

"Good, good," Latigo said. "Then that only leaves the one problem."

"And what is that?"

"You need to speak to the marshal and convince him to let me go find that man."

She balked at the notion. "Me? Why me?"

"I told you, he spent a lot of time looking for the identity of the possible partner to the man who was killed. He did that to help Glen, but it was mostly as a favor to you."

Cleo appeared to have an inner war for a few seconds. "Yes . . . well . . . uh, I'll be sure and thank him when I see him."

"You have to do more than thank him, Miss Van Ness. You must get him to let me go find this Yancy Pine. He knows I'm more than capable, that I know every nook or hiding place between Mother Earth and Father Sky. But he is a deputy U.S. marshal. There is no provision in his code of honor that allows him to let a prisoner run loose. He might need a little special coaxing"—he displayed a surreptitious smile—"if you follow my drift."

Cleo understood, all right. She frowned at him and then wrinkled her brow in thought, glancing at her brother. He and her father were standing close together, separated by the steel bars, speaking in low tones. The anxiety and dread in her father's face matched the worry and terror in that of her brother. She needed Latigo to help save Glen from a jail sentence and possibly death by a hangman's noose.

"I'll convince him," she promised. "Where is he?"

"He headed off to get some sleep—the tanner's extra room around back. He isn't due back at the jail till late this afternoon."

She took a deep breath and let it out slowly. "I'll go see him," she vowed. Then she hurried over to speak to Glen and her father.

Latigo smiled and remembered back to how awkward he had been when he met the woman he would marry. So many dreams and plans. He had tried to farm, and then an extended drought ruined the crop. He had hired on for a ranch, only to hurt his back the first week and end up unable to sit on a horse for a month. Even the job at the local saloon had brought too much strife into their life. The pay was so little, he had tried to gamble and win enough to survive. When he was let go because the mining town went broke, he had been at his wit's end. It was starve or beg, so he had robbed a wealthy gent of enough to buy some food. It was the beginning of the end of a normal life.

Thinking back, he shouldn't have been so proud. What pride was there in being a thief? It would have been better to humble himself and ask for help. Now he had a chance to make a difference in a young man's life; he had to do this.

Cleo summoned her courage as she hurried over to the back of the tanner's shop. She went to the door of the dwelling and rapped on it smartly with her knuckles. It was loud and hard, intended to wake him, if Wes happened to be asleep.

There came a mutter or grunt of discontent from the other side. The door suddenly opened, and a shirtless Wes Gavin stood before her, towel in hand, freshly shaven, his hair damp from being washed, and a sprinkle of moisture glistening on his bare chest.

Cleo was dumbstruck at the sight. She had caught Wes cleaning up, and doing a rather thorough job too from the looks of it.

"Miss Van Ness?" the marshal queried, regarding her with a puzzled frown.

"Um, Mr. Latigo said you would be naked—" She gasped, realizing her blunder, and hastily corrected, "I mean *sleeping!*"

He did not respond to her slip, nor make sport of the crimson flush that immediately colored her complexion. "I didn't have much luck trying to catch a nap, so I decided to wash up instead," he told her, pausing to run the towel over his chest and about his neck to dry himself.

Cleo finally gathered her wits about her and averted her gaze, finding a new interest in staring at the toes of her shoes.

"Mr. Latigo told me how you found a wanted circular on the gambler my brother killed and his friend."

"They fit the handbill description," he replied, dropping the towel and slipping on his shirt. He waited, forcing her to continue.

"Yes, well, Mr. Latigo said he knew how to find the man. I offered to send Emmett with him so they could track the gambler's partner down and bring him back here." Cleo was babbling, but couldn't seem to find a stopping point. "Mr. Latigo thought, and I agreed, that there's

a good chance that Yancy character will have the gun—
the one Glen said the gambler was carrying." She took a
breath, having rattled on inanely, before finishing. "If not,
he might confess to having taken it after the shooting."

"Latigo is his first name, Miss Van Ness. You needn't
put a *mister* in front of it."

She lifted her eyes, careful to stare only at the man's
face, while her chagrin was replaced with irritation. "All
right. I don't remember his last name, okay? And I know
I sound like some kind of ranting idiot, but I'm asking
you to let him help find the dead gambler's partner."

Wes buttoned his shirt and then rubbed his freshly
shaven chin. "I don't know if I can do that. Latigo Dykes
is my prisoner and my responsibility."

"He promised me he would find the man and return.
And Emmett would be with him. I'm sure the two of
them can do this."

"You mistake my concern, lady," he told her seriously. "I don't want the old boy to get hurt. He saved my
hide, and I owe him."

The news was unexpected, but she continued with
her mission. "Latigo volunteered to help, so he could
save an innocent man from prison or worse. I think that
is worth the risk."

"It would leave me shorthanded for guarding the jail,"
Wes pointed out.

"I'll have Kip and his two pals come in to help. They
seem to think you are about the best thing to arrive in
Sunset since the first saloon was opened."

Wes chuckled at the news and then asked, "So what
do I get out of this?"

Cleo bridled. "You get to save an innocent man from going to prison!"

"You saw how warm and friendly Dee was this morning, and she only wanted a story. I would think this would be worth something to you too."

"What?" Cleo was aghast at his insinuation. "You expect me to . . . to . . ." she sputtered, "to barter my favors for your cooperation?"

"Well, since you brought it up . . ." He dangled the line.

"I didn't bring it up. You did!" she fumed. "And I have considerably more ethics and dignity than Delight Johnson. I'm not in the habit of offering my wares to a man to garner his help or support."

"I understand your point of view," he conceded, but went on dryly. "Besides, with you being such a proper lady and all, I doubt you have any idea how to actually kiss a man. I apologize for even bringing it up."

Cleo glowered at him. "I'm not completely ignorant of how to kiss a man! But I won't be taunted or tricked into kissing anyone."

"Like I said, I shouldn't have brought it up. After all, Dee didn't actually kiss me on the mouth; a peck on the cheek doesn't mean anything."

"It did to her!" Cleo exploded. "That backstabbing little twit has chased after every guy I've shown an interest in since we were kids. She was trying to show me that she could have you too, if she wanted."

"I ought to have something to say about that, shouldn't I?"

"You don't know her. She's crafty and sneaky. She's

half coyote and half weasel. She never meets anything head-on; it's always from the side or behind."

"So I shouldn't read anything into her kissing me."

"You just said it was not a real kiss," Cleo reminded him curtly.

Wes scrunched up a hurt look. "Maybe not, but it was the closest thing I've gotten from an honest to goodness lady in a long time. That makes it pretty special."

"Lady!" Cleo cried. "She's a devious, backstabbing vixen!"

"That seems a little harsh. After all, she is a respectable member of the community and a reporter for the town newspaper."

Cleo abruptly stepped forward, slid a hand up behind Wes' head for leverage, and planted a heated kiss right on his mouth. It wasn't too lengthy or impassioned, but it definitely made a statement. She pulled away before he could reach out and ensnare her in his arms.

"*That*, Marshal Gavin, is a kiss!" she exclaimed, suddenly short of breath.

Wes grinned, his expression showing both surprise and satisfaction. "You'll get no argument from me, lady."

Cleo was unable to slow her heart rate or suck enough air into her lungs. Irate at herself and the absurd situation, she blurted out: "Now that I've humbled myself to the same elevation as Delight Johnson, will you please let Latigo go search for that other gambler?"

"It never entered my mind to stop him," Wes admitted easily. "Tell him I wish him luck and I'll expect him back in a few days."

Cleo felt a sudden shift in her temperament, from livid to stunned. "Then . . . so you . . ." she sputtered. "You made me kiss you for nothing!"

Wes chuckled. "It wasn't for nothing. It's the best reward I ever got for doing something I was already going to do."

Laughing at her was not the smartest thing to do. Fortunately, Wes had good reflexes. When Cleo swung her open palm at his cheek, he ducked and stepped back out of reach.

"Hold back your fit of temper, lady!" he exclaimed. "You're the one who kissed me!"

"You honey-fuggled me into it!" Cleo snapped, stomping her foot furiously. "That's about as low-down and underhanded as a man can get."

Another smile, this time aimed at her rancor. "You have very pretty eyes when you're fired up," he commented. "Brings color to your cheeks too."

"You're a complete scoundrel," she huffed, spinning about. Then she stormed off down the street.

Chapter Nine

Latigo had led the marshal's horse to the jail. He would be riding it in case he happened to run into some of the Quinteen gang. It wouldn't have been a happy encounter if they recognized one of their own horses. Shep stepped out onto the street to wish him well on his search, when a man suddenly appeared, having come from the alleyway. To both of their surprise, he had a gun trained on them.

"Latigo Dykes, I'm told you call yourself." The man sneered the words. "Well, I went to a lot of trouble to find you, and I know who you really are . . . *Mr. Gentleman Bandit!*"

Shep threw a curious look at Latigo and asked, "Who did he say you are?"

Latigo's past had caught up with him at the worst possible time. He ignored Shep's question, taking a side-step so the part-time sheriff would not be in the line of fire.

"I recognize you too," he replied with a calm he didn't feel. "You're the crooked banker from Cherry Creek— Nathan Hawks."

Nathan curled his lips. "I told you I'd hunt you down. No one robs me twice and gets away with it, you filthy thief."

"You're the thief, stealing people's homes and farms, charging them such high interest, they end up broke."

"Yeah, funny how that goes," Nathan growled back. "Both times, after you robbed me, one of those damn farmers arrived and paid off his loan in full."

"At 30 percent interest, you had already been paid twice for those places."

"What I do is legal," Nathan argued. "They sign a note, and the rate of interest is right in front of them, printed in black and white. It's no fault of mine if some of them are too dumb to understand what they're signing."

"I don't care who you are," Shep interjected carefully. "You best put that gun away, mister."

"You keep your nose out of this, youngster, or you might end up lying in the street next to this no-good highwayman."

"The man is already under arrest," Shep tried again. "A deputy U.S. marshal brought him in, along with two other wanted men."

The news caused Nathan to snicker. "Oh, yeah, as if I'm going to believe he is under arrest when he's standing there with a gun on his hip!" He aimed down the barrel of his gun. "I've got a copy of the wanted poster on this guy, and it reads DEAD OR ALIVE." He snorted. "I'm going to take the easy way and make him dead."

Latigo nodded to Shep. "You stay out of this, son. It has nothing to do with you."

"I'm the sheriff," Shep objected.

"I don't want your death on my conscience." Latigo

heaved a sigh. "I already owe you more of a debt than I can ever pay back."

Shep was now thoroughly confused. "What are you talking about?"

"Step away from the bandit, Sheriff," the banker warned, growing tired of the chatter. "I've no quarrel with you."

"Do like he says, Shep. Believe me when I say I'm not worth your getting hurt."

Shep took one step toward the jail, but he kept one hand on the butt of his pistol. Latigo feared he might still try to save him.

"Give me a minute before you shoot, Hawks. There's something I have to tell this fellow. Once I say my piece, you can do whatever you feel you have to."

"Best talk fast," he answered. "I've lost all patience with you."

Latigo gazed over at Shep. Shep was completely baffled by the situation. In a moment his confusion would become a bitter hatred. Better for Shep to hate him than to risk his life trying to save him.

"I'm Latigo Dykes today, Shep, but before I became that man, I was known as Jack Donahue." He paused to let the words sink in. "Shep . . . son"—he struggled to finish the sentence—"I'm the man who ran out on you and your mother. I let Jack Donahue die a good many years ago and became who I am today. All I can say is, I'm durned ashamed of what I did—and that's the gospel truth."

Wes had slept some while guarding the prisoners during the night, so he didn't try napping after Cleo's visit.

He went down and dropped off his dirty clothes to get them cleaned. When he stepped out of the laundry, he spied Latigo standing with his hands raised. Shep was near the building, and a third man held a gun on Latigo.

Wes strode forward quickly, closing to within fifty feet before the unknown man noticed him. The gunman turned his head but kept the gun pointed at Latigo.

"Hold it right there, fella!" he commanded, lifting his left hand, palm facing outward, in a *stop* motion. "This here don't concern you."

"You've got a pistol pointed at my deputy," Wes replied. "That makes it my concern."

"He's a wanted man—the Gentleman Bandit, they call him."

"I know all about it," Wes said.

"Easy, Marshal," Latigo warned. "This is Nathan Hawks, a bloodsucking banker I robbed two different times. He's mad over me giving money to a couple of farmers he was about to foreclose on. He lost a chance to grab their land and homes because of me. He'd as soon shoot you as look at you."

"Well, he can't shoot you, because you're in my custody!"

"What kind of moron do you take me for?" Nathan howled his rage. "This guy can't be your deputy and your prisoner both!"

"Lower your gun, and I'll explain it to you."

But he wasn't of a mind to listen. "I'm going to put a hole through his black heart, and then, if you really are a lawman, you can take charge of his body. I'm not even after the reward."

Wes had his right hand on the butt of his gun and used his left to point at the badge he was wearing.

"Take a look at this before you do something you won't live to regret!" He edged his words with ice, taking special notice that the banker held a pistol that required he first cock back the hammer before he could shoot. "I really am a deputy U.S. marshal, Mr. Hawks, and I'm giving you fair warning. If you make the slightest effort to slip your thumb up to cock that pistol, I'll kill you before you can pull the trigger."

Hawks glowered at him, but his aim didn't waver. "You can't bluff me, Marshal. I judge the worth of men every day for a living."

"If you are a good judge of character, you'd best take a second look. I'm not a man given to bluffing."

"Don't risk your life for me," Latigo told Wes. "I've sinned enough in this life to pay the ultimate price. You don't have to—"

But Nathan made his choice at that instant. He quickly thumbed back the hammer so he could pull the trigger—

Wes used his practiced draw and all of his speed. He fired twice as quickly as he could, both bullets striking the crooked banker in the chest. The man was too stunned by the sudden impact of two bullets entering his body to squeeze the trigger. He sank to the ground without getting off his own shot.

"Damn fool," Wes muttered, knowing he had ended the man's life.

Latigo lowered his hands and stood with his shoulders sagging, head ducked low, while Shep moved over and checked Nathan for any sign of life.

"You should have let him pull the trigger," Latigo said. "I've been a bandit for fifteen years. I told you I was ready to pay for all those robberies."

Wes suffered regret over having ended a man's life, fraudulent and greed-driven or not, and holstered his gun. He moved over next to Latigo and stared down at the man he had killed. "You said he was stealing people's land?"

"It was legal, providing you call charging 30 percent interest legal. He used the ignorance of people against them, offering to be lenient on payments and such. Before the victims realized how much their loan was costing them, they were so far in debt, they couldn't pay." Latigo sighed. "I managed to save a couple of families, but he ruined dozens of others and was growing rich."

"Yet he came after you."

Latigo snorted his contempt. "The black-hearted snake had more pride than sense. He claimed that no one ever got the best of Nathan Hawks—not ever. He was so blasted arrogant, he didn't even hire someone else to do the job of hunting me down. He wanted to kill me himself."

Before Wes could say anything more, Dee came running across the street. She had her notebook tightly clasped in her hand. He tipped his head toward his waiting horse. "You'd best get started for the Van Ness ranch. If I read Cleo right, Emmett will be ready to ride before you get there."

"I'm sorry about this, Marshal. I really am."

"Get going, before Dee grabs you to get your account of the fight."

Latigo caught up his horse. He mounted and paused

to look down at Shep. "I'm durn sorry, son," he said quietly. "For everything."

Shep didn't reply but motioned to a man who was standing nearby. "Help me get this body over to the carpenter's place. I'll send off a wire to his hometown and see what they want done for him."

"He wasn't a popular man." Latigo spoke to Wes. "But I think he has a married sister. She can probably close out or sell his bank." With that said, he turned his horse for the main road and started off to the Van Ness ranch.

Dee planted herself in front of Wes as Shep and a second man lifted the banker's body and began to cart him away. Her pencil was out and ready.

"I saw what happened from the porch," she said with a mixture of excitement and shock. "I—that was the second man I've seen killed right in front of my eyes."

"It's not a pretty sight," Wes said.

"No, but I can't help being impressed."

"Impressed?"

"That man had his gun pointed at Latigo. How did you manage to shoot him before he pulled the trigger?"

"He hadn't cocked the pistol yet."

She uttered a sigh of disbelief. "Still, that was the quickest draw I ever saw. And the two shots sounded more like one, being that they were fired so close together."

"A single shot doesn't always stop a man from pulling the trigger," Wes explained. "I fired twice to try to ensure he didn't get off his own shot."

"What was he, a robber, a hired killer, a bounty hunter?"

"He was a banker."

Dee pulled a face. "You killed a banker?" She gave her head a shake. "Are you sure you're in the right profession? You make a prisoner your deputy, and then you kill a banker who is out to kill a bandit."

Wes explained what he knew about the man and how Latigo had crossed his path twice to save the farms of two families. Then he told her he had warned the man not to try to cock his pistol. When his thumb moved, he had no choice but to stop him.

When Dee finished scribbling, her expression brightened. "I don't think I'll ever get used to seeing someone killed."

"Be a sorry state if people ever get so dull-minded that they could watch a shooting and not get sick inside."

"On the plus side," she said, her chipper self again, "everything I've written since you arrived in town has been published in the Denver paper. I'm getting more writing exposure than I had ever hoped—all because of you."

"I'm happy to be such a windfall for your career," Wes commented cynically.

She laughed. "It isn't all bad. You are getting quite a reputation too."

"I'm not looking for a reputation," he grumbled. But her exuberance forced him to exude a tight grin. "However, I'm glad that my encounters here have helped you with your writing goals."

She returned to business. "Where did Mr. Dykes go?"

"He is running an errand, and I wouldn't want it in the paper." When her eyebrows drew together skeptically, he added, "I'll tell you all about it when it's safe to print."

"I'll hold you to that, Marshal."

"Now, if you'll excuse me, I have to wire the head office and tell them what happened—before they read about it in the local newspaper."

Dee flashed a final smile and whirled about. She scampered away like a frisky colt, hurrying off to write her story.

Latigo's enthusiasm for hunting down the missing gambler had waned. The shooting of Nathan Hawks weighed heavily on his shoulders. True, the man was an underhanded sneak, one who coaxed people into borrowing more than they could ever pay back. His dealings enabled him to steal their land and sell it for a huge profit. And he would have killed Latigo in cold blood. Still, his death had come about because Latigo had robbed him twice. Justified or not, by his gun or that of the marshal, he had killed the banker.

He arrived at the Van Ness ranch to find Emmett in the yard, packing supplies on the back of his horse. Cleo was on the porch, along with her father and mother.

"Thought you might have changed your mind," Emmett greeted him.

"Had a little trouble in town before I left. Dee was on the scene, so I'm sure it will be in the next newsletter. I'll tell you about it on the trail."

"I'm ready to go," Emmett said, climbing aboard his horse. "Any idea how long this will take?"

"Yancy has no reason to think anyone would come after him, so I don't think he will be too hard to find. With luck, only a few days."

"You do this for us, and we'll owe you a real favor, Mr. Dykes," Ogden said from the porch.

"Yes," his wife chimed in, "anything you need, you only have to ask."

Cleo moved over to stand by his horse. Her expression was one of dark concern. "This trouble, it didn't involve Marshal Gavin?"

"He's all right," Latigo told her. "It was something from my past. You'll read about it, but Wes is just fine."

Emmett swung his horse over next to Latigo as they rode out of the yard. "Which way we headed?" he asked.

"We'll start at the nearest gambling spot and work our way around until we pick up Yancy's trail. A man like him won't be hard to follow."

"I'm with you—for however long it takes," Emmett vowed. "Cleo says that Glen swears the shooting was self-defense. We've got to bring that man in to prove it."

Latigo experienced a reinvigoration from Emmett's eagerness. He felt a little better, knowing he was on a quest to save an innocent man from being sent to prison or hanged. He had seen the shock, and then disgust, on Shep's face, but this could help change that. A good deed couldn't make up for the years of family neglect and his banditry, but it was a step in the right direction.

Chapter Ten

Wes was at the jail when Shep returned from having sent off the wires. The young man appeared troubled, with puzzlement and anguish etched into his features, although he didn't voice his feelings.

"I contacted the U.S. Marshals' office for you and sent the message you wrote," he announced.

"What about the banker?"

"The telegraph operator knew him personally. He said he would inform Nathan's sister, but there was no love lost between them. Plus it seems Nathan had swindled about everyone in town at one time or another. The operator said his only close friends were in the form of gold coin or paper money, and he kept them locked in his safe." With a cynical grunt, he added, "Doesn't sound like his leaving this earth was much of a loss to humanity."

"Hated to have to shoot him, but he was going to kill Latigo."

Shep hesitated, as if he might say something about that, but instead returned to their present situation. "I spoke to Emmett, and he promised to send some men from the ranch to help guard our three guests," Shep told Wes. "Seems a little strange: he named the very same three guys who tried to take Glen out of here by force."

"Reckon those boys had a change of heart."

"I see Latigo left on your horse. That's a good idea, in case they happened to meet up with a Quinteen rider along the way. Wouldn't want anyone recognizing one of their own horses." Wes nodded, and Shep asked, "You really think Latigo can find the dead man's partner?"

"He knows every place a gambling man can disappear in for a hundred miles around. If anyone can locate him, it will be Lat."

"He told me right off that he was your prisoner, although he never said why you had arrested him. You knew he was the Gentleman Bandit, and yet you trusted him to guard the jail here by himself."

"Lat might be a bandit, but he's an honest man. He gave me his word."

"Did you know he was my father?"

Wes decided to go with the truth. "That's the reason we came here, Shep." Then he went on to tell him about catching the man, and how Latigo had helped capture the Quinteen brothers. He finished with, "Latigo had the idea of giving you the reward money from the two killers. It was the only thing he asked of me."

"He left us when I was just a kid."

"Yes, he told me how he panicked when he couldn't put food on the table. He said that was the only time he ever stole from someone who didn't deserve it."

"My wife and kids are all fond of him." His voice grew cold. "I was fond of him!"

"Once your wagon wheel slips into a ditch, it can be real hard to pull out again. That's what happened to Lat."

"Think he'll have to go to prison?"

"I'll be putting in a good word for him, but he'll probably have to spend some time behind bars."

The two of them conversed for a spell until a rap came at the door. After Wes called to "come ahead," the door opened, and Joe Fremont, the liveryman, appeared. He didn't hesitate but stepped inside and closed the door.

"Marshal . . . Shep," he greeted them both. "I thought you ought to know about some strangers who arrived a short bit ago."

"Speak up, Joe," Shep encouraged.

"Two men, hard-looking fellows, both with killer's eyes and packing a week's worth of dust." He put his attention on Wes. "They come to the livery and seen those Quinteen mounts you rode in with—suppose you know Latigo took your mount. Anyways, they commenced to ask about the Quinteen boys. Well, sir, I didn't tell them squat, not until they fessed up to being bounty hunters. Then I told them they might as well start tracking some of the rest of the gang, 'cause you had two of them already in jail."

"How'd they take the news?" Wes asked him.

"That's why I come over here to see you," he said. "They showed some interest but not one ounce of regret or disappointment." Fremont gathered his brow into a frown. "Now, what kind of joker spends days or weeks on a wanted man's trail and then shrugs when he discovers someone else has claimed the prize? If it was me, I'd have growled and complained for no less than thirty minutes."

"There are other gang members running loose," Shep pointed out.

"Yes, but a fair share of the bounty is out of their reach."

"They try and get any other information?"

"Asked about the prison wagon, but I said I didn't know anything about that."

"Where are they now?" Shep asked.

"They headed over to the Silver Dollar for a drink. I waited until they were inside before I brought you the news."

"You're a good man, Fremont," Wes told him. "Those two might not have been disappointed because they have an idea as to where the other gang members are."

"I don't know, Wes. If a couple bounty hunters caught up with you, the other Quinteens might not be far behind," Shep said. "Could one of those guys actually be a relation to the two boys we got in the cell?"

The liveryman grunted in answer to the question. "One appears to be either Mexican or have some Indian blood, and the other is a lanky sort with dirty, mustard-colored hair. Don't fit at all with the two boys you brought in."

Wes agreed. "You're right. Most of the Quinteen family have rusty-colored hair and enough freckles to paint the side of a house. At least, the ones I've come across are all cut from the same bolt of cloth."

"I'll be getting back," Fremont said.

"Thanks again for the warning. We'll keep our eyes open."

As soon as Fremont had left, Shep went to the window and peered out into the street. "You want me to check it out?" he asked. "After all, the Quinteens are your prisoners, not mine."

"I don't think a bunch of killer outlaws will take that into account. A lawman is a lawman in their book."

"One of us ought to get a look at them."

Shep was right, but he had no experience in sizing men up. Besides which, Wes was familiar with a good number of bounty hunters. He might recognize them by sight or name.

"I'll step over and take a gander at them. You watch our guests and keep the scattergun handy."

"You got it, Wes."

Walking down to the Silver Dollar, Wes entered the saloon and paused to allow his eyes to adjust to the darker interior. It was early afternoon and Sunday to boot, so the place was nearly empty. The barkeep was just exiting the room by the rear door, carrying a box of empty bottles. Two men were standing at one end of the bar, each with a nearly empty mug of beer in front of him. With the bartender out back, there were only the three of them in the room.

Wes wandered over to the pair and gave them a quick once-over. The taller man was lean and wiry. His natural squint glowed with suspicion from under bushy brows. The shorter gent had a dark complexion, black hair to his shoulders, and the unblinking eyes of a snake. He was compact in build but no more than four inches over five feet.

"Howdy, boys," Wes greeted them.

They continued to eye him closely, but the tall man mustered up an artificial smile. "How-do, pard. You looking for us?"

"The stableman said you were bounty hunters."

"That's right. Guess we got here too late. We were told two of the Quinteen boys were already in jail." He showed a curious expression. "That your doing?"

"Yep," Wes replied. "But it still leaves four or five more running loose. You thinking of going after them—all by yourselves?"

"We'll try to cull the herd a little at a time before we take on the he-bull, the one called Hyrum. Hear tell he's the toughest of the bunch."

Wes didn't hide his amazement. "There's a sizable bounty on the whole bunch, but it's a risky job for only two men."

"You the sheriff here in Sunset?" the smaller man asked.

"Not me. I'm a deputy U.S. marshal. I've got two Quinteens as my prisoners."

"You're Gavin?"

At his affirmative nod, the two men exchanged glances. It was a mere flicker between them, but it did not escape Wes' attention. The tall one quickly covered his interest and presented a concerned expression.

"We have heard of you, the man who brought in Jay

Quinteen to be hanged," the darker-complexioned man said.

"Yeah, I've got to hand it to you, Marshal," the tall one remarked. "You're warning us, while you are riding with a cocked pistol in your waistband. After being responsible for Lark's eldest son being hanged," he elaborated, "I wouldn't set foot within a hundred miles of any of the Quinteen family."

"What are your names?" Wes changed the subject. "Maybe I've heard of you."

"We're new in this part of the country," he answered.

"It's true," his partner agreed. "We've been down in Texas for the past few years. They are short of lawmen, so there is plenty of work."

"Well, you seem to know I'm deputy marshal Wes Gavin. So who are you?"

The taller one shrugged. "I go by Sentry. My pard here is Rojas."

"That's better than both of you claiming your name is Smith."

Sentry laughed. "When you manhunt for a living, you don't use your family names. It's not exactly a well-thought-of profession."

"It's true," Rojas agreed. "Look at you, running around with a target on your back for taking Jay Quinteen in to be hanged. If you had a family, they might be in danger of the Quinteen gang doing them harm to get even."

Wes gave them a closer scrutiny. "Seems I spotted a dodger on a couple of hardcase gunmen. They pulled a couple jobs around the Denver area. There were no names listed, but you two fit the description given."

Both men stiffened ever so slightly, but these were professionals, not given to panic. Sentry displayed an insolent smirk. "That wasn't us, Marshal. We're making a living catching crooks and thieves. We're helping you do your job."

Rojas jeered, "Yes, we are like so many others. Who can say who is who?"

Wes grinned. "You're right, of course. Being a lawman, I see a dozen men a day that fit the description of men on wanted posters."

The two laughed without mirth.

"So, do you boys want to talk to the two Quinteens in the jail?" Wes asked carefully. If he could get them to enter the jail, Shep would be ready to get the drop on them. Then he would do some real checking on their background. He added innocently, "They might give you an idea about the whereabouts of their gang."

Sentry's eyebrows arched at the offer. "You'd let us do that?"

"Anything you can do to keep those fellows from catching up with me would be appreciated."

But just when Wes thought he might have coaxed them into a trap, Rojas narrowed his dark eyes.

"Yes, and we would also be a single step away from ending up in a cell."

Wes started to protest the man's accurate deduction, but things turned suddenly violent.

Rojas launched a fist at his head. Wes ducked under

the blow and grabbed for his gun. He was too slow, as Sentry charged into him from his gun side!

Wes caught hold of Sentry and whirled to one side, using his hip to lift the guy off his feet. As he spun, he sent Sentry rolling over the top of a table. Before he could get his feet set, Rojas landed a solid shot to his jaw and followed with another that caught him above his right eye. Wes regained his balance and struck back, smashing the shorter man flush in the mouth. An instant pain lanced across his knuckles from making contact with the man's teeth, but Rojas didn't so much as flinch from the blow.

He came back at once, wading forward, fists flying so fast, Wes could only try to block and cover up from the numerous blows. He could have worn the man down, except Sentry rejoined the fight. Being hammered from two sides at once, Wes couldn't avoid every punch. He tasted blood and was dazed when a fist slammed solidly against his temple.

The world spun before his eyes, and Wes could not maintain his balance. Deluged by the violent attack of rock-hard fists pounding his body, he sank to his knees. A solid boot kicked him in the ribs, and the wind was driven from his lungs. He knew if he fell to the floor, these two would kick him to death, but he had no escape. Another boot exploded against his head. Amid the ensuing blackness, bolts of light flashed before his eyes. He feared this moment would be the last he would ever know.

Suddenly there came a gasp, a cry of surprise, and the pounding ceased. Wes sagged against the bar counter, his arms still up to protect himself. But the attack had stopped.

Through blurred vision and a groggy thought process,

he spied a big man, taller than Sentry by several inches and built like a walking outhouse. It was Scat.

Rojas left his feet as one of Scat's huge paws jerked him up like a ten-pound sack of spuds. He tossed the man fifteen feet across the room, where he bounced off a table and slammed into the wall.

Sentry did something stupid: he hit the big Van Ness ranch hand in the face. Scat barely blinked, and retaliated with his own punch. The force behind the blow was that of a double jackhammer. Sentry reeled backward through the batwing doors and landed on his back in the street.

"You okay?" Scat asked, hunkering down in front of Wes. "I just rode in to help guard the prisoners. Emmett sent me."

Wes tried to answer, but his brain was not yet communicating with his mouth. He wanted to tell the man to grab Rojas and Sentry, to not let them get away. But by the time he recovered his wits enough to speak, Rojas had scrambled out of the room. Moments later, as air entered back into his lungs, two horses raced out of town, and Wes cursed himself for making a tenderfoot mistake.

The array of bright lights ricocheting about in his head finally dimmed enough for him to get his vocal function working again. "Thanks, Scat. I got careless. If you hadn't come along, I might have—well, you saw how good I was doing against those two."

Scat grinned. "I kind of hated to step in, the way you were manhandling that pair."

"Yeah, had them right where they wanted me."

Scat laughed and then grew serious. "You able to walk? I 'spect you need to lie down and get some rest."

Wes shook out his shoulders and rose unsteadily to his feet. He used the tips of his fingers to test the bruising about his face. There were a couple of tender places, some swelling above one eye, and a lump near his jaw. His ribs were sore, and they hurt with each breath, but he didn't feel any sharp, jabbing pain; that was good news. If Scat had been a few seconds later, his next rest would have taken place inside a pine box.

"I must be getting old, 'cause I'm feeling a mite unsteady, Scat. I wonder if you could lend a hand and help me over to my room."

Scat didn't hesitate putting an arm around Wes. He hefted him high enough that his feet barely touched the ground and practically carried him out to the street.

"I'm grateful you showed up when you did," he told the solidly built brute.

"It's no big deal, Marshal. Emmett and Miss Cleo said we was to help guard the jail while Emmett and your helper were gone. Kip took my horse to the livery while I stopped and spoke to Shep. Pepper is kind of stove-up, so I think he's going to stick at the ranch another day or two. It was Shep who told me I ought to check and see how you were doing."

"I'm obliged to both of you. I only wish you'd arrived a few minutes earlier. I figured those two might have been part of the Quinteen gang, but then I remembered seeing a handbill on them—a couple of petty crooks from over on the eastern slope some years back."

"What was they doing here?"

"They claimed to be bounty hunters." Wes grunted. "I suppose they could have changed professions. According to the dodger, they weren't very successful as criminals."

"Seeing how they got here second, chasing after the Quinteen boys, it don't look as if they are doing any better at a manhunt."

"Well, whatever they were here for, I'm thanking you for stepping in to save my hide."

Scat said, "I know I ain't the smartest guy around, but any time there's a fight, I'm usually on the winning side."

Wes grimaced with pain from every step but asked, "How'd you come by the name of Scat?"

"From the times when I joined in during a brawl," he said. "Real name is Leroy Upton, but most guys start yelling at one another to 'scatter' or 'scat' when I show up. My friends know that when they are in trouble, they only have to call the 'Scat man,' and the fight is over." He chuckled. "After a tussle or two, they dropped the *man* part and just call me Scat now."

"Well, you certainly proved your worth to me."

"We didn't know how long you would need help watching the jail," Scat said, still supporting much of Wes' weight for the walk toward the tanner's shop. "When is the prison wagon due?"

"I wired them to hold off until the judge arrived for Glen's trial," Wes explained. "When I saw the dead gambler had a wanted notice on him, I wired the judge and told him to hold off coming too. I thought I'd better wait for things to play out in Glen's case."

"Yeah, I see. Emmett told us he was leaving with the

old codger, the one who come to town with you. He's what—some kind of deputy?"

Before Wes could answer, Dee arrived. As usual, she had a notepad and pencil in her hands.

"What happened to you, Marshal?" she cried. "Who beat you up?"

"It's nothing serious," Wes answered.

"Nothing serious! You look like you jumped in between two mules during a kicking contest!"

"I got careless with a couple of jaspers who were wanted by the law. Scat here ran them off."

Dee was trying to scribble and walk alongside him at the same time. "Who were they? Was it part of the Quinteen gang?"

"Not according to the dodger I read."

"So what happened? Tell me how you got into a fight with them. Did they ambush you? How did Scat get involved? Are they coming back?"

"Great day in the morning, Delight Johnson," he blurted out, groaning at once from the amount of effort required. "You fire off questions faster than a jackleg lawyer at a talking convention."

She shot him a sharp look and stopped in her tracks. However, she was forced to hurry to catch up when Scat and Wes didn't stop walking.

"I don't care to be called Delight," she fumed, waving her pencil at his head. "And I need answers so I can write a story of what happened."

Wes gathered up an extra breath and replied, "I bungled an arrest of two men who matched a description on a wanted notice. Scat here arrived to save me from getting my head bashed in. Now I'm on my way to get some bunk time. After a few hours of rest, I hope I'll be able to walk under my own power." He put a hard stare on her. "Is that good enough for you?"

She snapped off her reply. "Yes. Thank you for your courtesy!" Then she whirled about and headed for the newspaper office.

"That there gal has got more spunk than a dozen month-old colts," Scat said. "And Miss Cleo seems to worry about you too. I'd say you've got a full plate of red ants and honey on both hands."

Wes tried a weak grin at the strange metaphor. "It's complicated, Scat," he said. "I'm for thinking my whole life has gotten downright complicated."

Chapter Eleven

Hyrum listened to Sentry's story. When he'd finished, he told him to go down to the creek and soak his swollen mouth and loosened teeth with a wet, cold rag. Rojas didn't look much better, walking stiffly and slightly bent over from being tossed against the wall of the saloon.

"From the looks of those two, the marshal sure enough has some help," Lark complained. "Six of us might not be enough to get the boys out."

"Sentry said the bartender told him the prison wagon hadn't been sent for yet."

"Unless the liveryman was making it up about Gavin hanging around for a trial of some rancher's kid."

"No reason for him to lie. He couldn't have known Sentry and Rojas were riding with us. The marshal mentioned a wanted notice with two men fitting their description, probably an old one from back before they joined up with us."

"He still knows we are looking for him, big brother.

He has to know we'll be coming. If he's found some help, we could be in for a real battle."

Hyrum rubbed the rusty-colored stubble on his chin thoughtfully. After a few moments of contemplation he made up his mind. "You're right. We ought to have some more help, and it would only take a day or two to get it."

"You mean Mort." Lark was on the same train of thought, considering their cousin and ex-partner. "He and his pals have stuck to rustling cattle and a few head of horses for the past couple years. Don't know if he would be all that happy trying to break my boys out when the town is full of deputies."

"It's our money that staked him when he was short of cash more than once. He owes us, and we're going to collect. Moab and Saul can ride over there and be back in a couple days. If Mort brings Hank and Whitey, we'll be nine against the marshal and whoever he has hired."

Lark gave an enthusiastic bob of his head. "I'll put some supplies together for them while you tell your boys what to do." As an afterthought, he added, "And I reckon the couple of days' rest will probably be good for Sentry and Rojas."

Hyrum grunted in response. He wanted plenty of help on this so he didn't wind up getting himself and his boys shot up. Sometimes Lark and his sons weren't worth the powder to blow them up. But they were family. He put his misgivings aside and walked over to talk to his boys.

Wes woke up at the sound of tapping at his door. He stiffly rose to a sitting position and blinked to clear a thick veil of fog that encompassed his thought process.

"Yeah?" he managed hoarsely.

The door was pushed open, and Dee came into the room. She had a tray in her hands with a bowl, some bread, and a cup on it. She explained her purpose at once.

"I didn't think you were up to getting your own meal tonight, so I made up a tray for you."

"You didn't have to—"

"No, don't thank me." She cut him short. "You've been nice enough to give me some stories to write. I'm only repaying the courtesy."

"I appreciate it regardless of the reason," he said.

Those words put a smile on her face. She used her elbow to push the door closed behind her, but it didn't swing all the way shut. Not concerned about their privacy, she moved over to the bed and placed the tray on his lap. Getting a look at him up close, she uttered a sigh.

"I should get some water and soak the swelling above your eye."

Wes picked up the cup of coffee and took a sip. The bowl held chili con carne, the bread was still warm, and the aroma smelled delicious.

"You didn't pick this up at Bertha's," he remarked. "Did you make this yourself?"

Dee blushed. "Well, I had to fix supper for the folks and me, so I made up an extra plate."

He tasted the chili and found it just spicy enough to stimulate his palate. "It's very good," he told her. "Makes me thankful those two polecats didn't knock my teeth out."

"I do most of the cooking at our house, although my mother is a good cook too. She runs the newspaper office and sets the print for the press. My father does most of the writing and editing. I'm usually the one with some time to spare." She lifted her shoulders in a shrug. "Actually, I had done very little meaningful writing until Glen shot that gambler. Being that I was there to witness the killing, I got to write the story. Then you gave me a nice follow-up— more than one, as it turned out."

"I'm glad my assorted adventures are giving you a chance to write what you enjoy."

"I'd love to be a writer for a big newspaper back east. Even the *Rocky Mountain News* over at Denver would be wonderful. It has a readership in the thousands, while we have less than a hundred. If not for some advertising and support from people like the Van Ness family, we would have gone broke right off."

"Even a small town needs a good newspaper."

"Yes, but my father writes most everything of conse-quence. Until the killing, my only contribution was news about a barn raising, an upcoming party or festival, or someone's new baby—that sort of thing."

"I can see where that wouldn't be very exciting."

She smiled brightly. "I thought I'd only get the one story about the shooting, but all that changed when you rode into town. I was there to see you run off the three Van Ness riders. You probably saved Shep's life. My fa-ther had been watching too, but I got to you first, and then you told me about judicial prejudice, so he had to let me write the follow-up story."

"That's only fair," he said.

She continued, "And today you tried to apprehend two outlaws and nearly got yourself killed. That is another article I'll get credit for. You are a wealth of news, Mr. Gavin."

"It's a comfort knowing that putting my life at risk and having my face used like some kind of punching pillow is serving your purpose."

Dee laughed. "You make me sound callous and cold-hearted. I didn't want you getting injured for a story. But it does seem as if you keep sticking your neck out at every opportunity."

"It's the least I can do to help you in your writing endeavors."

Another short laugh, but she grew serious again. "There is one thing I'm curious about."

"Only one?"

She smiled. "Why are the very same three men you faced that first day now in town to help you guard the jail? I asked Kip this afternoon, but he only said it was their duty."

"They're good boys at heart," he said simply. "We just had to reach an understanding."

"You have a way about you, don't you?"

"Huh?" was his well-chosen reply.

"I mean, you capture bad men, you back down three men with guns and convert them into allies, and Latigo—I don't know what to think of him. He started out as your prisoner, and now he is trying to clear Glen's name."

"If I'm such a wizard at charming people," he said, "maybe I should have used a little more charm with those two guys this afternoon."

Dee allowed the subject to drop but continued to talk about trivial things while he ate. Wes finished off the chili with little effort. He didn't speak again until he had drunk the last of the coffee. Then he offered Dee the best smile his swollen face could muster.

"Thank you for bringing me supper, Miss Johnson. It was very tasty, and I truly appreciate it."

Dee leaned over the bed, her face only inches from his. "This is the only way I can see you in private. After all, you never took me up on the offer for a walk or a picnic. You're a man; I'm a woman." She regarded him with a coy look. "No telling where an outing together would lead."

"It would lead to trouble—with a capital *T*!" A voice from the doorway chipped the words off like ice shards.

Cleo stormed into the room and glowered at Dee. The girl at Wes' side jumped to her feet and spun about to glare right back.

"Don't you knock before entering a man's bedroom, Cleopatra?"

"You're getting careless about your conquests, Delight. You left the door ajar." She bore into Dee with a molten stare. "That's pretty careless, when I'm sure you wouldn't want anyone to see how you behave in private."

Dee put her hands on her hips but held a tight rein on her emotions. "Speaking of private, I believe it would be prudent if we were to speak outside."

Wes sat there in wonder as the two girls left the room. It was painful reaching over to set down the tray, but he managed to get the job done without crying out. Then he sagged back against his pillow and wondered if the two girls were going to tear each other's hair out. He certainly hoped not. They were both too pretty and well bred to be fighting. He heaved a weary sigh and waited to see which one would come through the door next.

Cleo walked a short distance, until they reached the alleyway. She took a quick look around to be sure they wouldn't be overheard and then whirled about to face Dee.

"What is it about you?" she demanded to know. "Why do you insist on going after everything or everyone I show the slightest bit of interest in?"

"Marshal Gavin is fair game," Dee replied firmly.

"I'm not talking just about him; it's everything."

"What are you talking about?"

Cleo took a deep breath to sooth her ire and gather a steadfast composure. "From the first time we met at school, you've done your darnedest to belittle me or be better than me at everything that came along. You compete with me at bake sales, dances, and at the town fair races, and you've chased after every guy who has ever said hello to me." She peered at her with a puzzled look and softened her voice. "Tell me the truth, Dee. What did I ever do to make you hate me so much?"

"I don't hate you," Dee replied, visibly taken aback by her sincerity.

"You must," Cleo argued. "Why else would you always try to best me at everything? Why go after any guy who gives me a second look?"

Dee shook her head. "It isn't like that. Besides, you're the one who started it."

"Me?"

"When school opened, you came along and took away half my friends. You've always had first choice of the guys because of your father and the fact that you are prettier than me."

"That's ridiculous!" Cleo scoffed her disdain. "I'm the one who's in your shadow when it comes to looks. And you're the smart one. You went to school before your family moved here. I only got to attend school for two years. When Mom came down with the fever, I had to stay home and tend to her and fix meals. She was left weakened for months, and I never got back to school. Do you have any idea how dumb I feel alongside you? Gracious, Dee! You write for a newspaper, while I can barely read."

An odd look entered Dee's expression, but her voice remained harsh. "You took Andy Jarvis away from me a couple of years back."

"Andy Jarvis?" Cleo laughed at the absurdity. "His father was forcing him to do the bookkeeping for their store, but he wanted to be a cowboy. The only reason he trailed after me was to get a chance to work on our ranch."

A stunned realization entered Dee's face. "That's why he left last year?"

"He went to work for a cattleman over near Raton. My father didn't want any hard feelings with Mr. Jarvis, so he wouldn't hire Andy."

"What about the Christmas dance, when you bought that fancy dress? I spent months saving up to buy a nice gown, and you showed up and stole the show!"

"Mother bought me the dress for my eighteenth birthday. I never had an occasion to wear it before that dance."

"We have a dance every month," Dee countered.

"Yes, but remember there was a traveling photographer in town for Christmas. Mother wanted to have me pose in my best dress. We had the picture taken an hour before the dance." She pulled a face. "Besides, how could I have known you would have a fancy dress for that one special night? After all, the only time you ever spoke to me was to insult me."

Dee appeared to swallow her irritation. "I . . . I thought you were doing everything to spite me, Cleo. From school, to Andy, to the dress, to always coming to town looking so pretty."

"It's just the opposite, Dee. I always thought you were the pretty one, and you were always considered a lady. I come from a ranch and grew up with two brothers. I have to dress up, or a good many people might think of me as a tomboy."

Dee lowered her head as if ashamed. "I didn't go after Emmett because of you," she murmured. "He is the one who came trying to court me."

"Yes, I know."

The girl's head lifted. "You know?"

"Emmett and I are good friends. He's told me a lot about you."

"What about Marshal Gavin?"

It was Cleo's turn to lower her head. "I . . . I don't know, Dee. I haven't been around him enough to know how I feel. Well, not really."

"You came into the room in a jealous rage," Dee maintained. "You acted as if I had taken a currycomb to your favorite horse."

Cleo's eyebrows drew together. "I may have overreacted a little."

"When I kissed him on the cheek, it was to spite you," Dee confessed. "He didn't know I was going to do it."

Cleo laughed at her admission. "Same here."

The comment caught Dee's attention. "You kissed him on the cheek too?"

Cleo exhaled markedly. "No. This time I really did want to get the better of you."

Dee displayed a sly simper. "You kissed him on the mouth," she deduced correctly. "I can't believe it. Emmett says you only let him kiss you one time, and that was after he had been courting you for several weeks."

"Yes, well, don't read too much into it. I'm sure Marshal Gavin didn't. It wasn't the same as a romantic kiss. More of a dare, actually."

"Hmm. How do you tell if a kiss is romantic or platonic?" At Cleo's frown, she clarified the unfamiliar word. "Romantic or a friendly peck on the lips."

"It wasn't a peck. I planted a good one on him."

Again Dee laughed, merrily this time. "Cleo, I think you and I have been missing out on a great friendship."

Cleo laughed too, and the two of them hugged. It was a sealing of a new relationship, one free of competition and backbiting. Somehow, Wes Gavin had been the unwitting catalyst for their becoming friends.

Wes was not surprised to see that the girl at the door was Cleo. After all, she worked around the ranch and had been blessed with two brothers. A girl with brothers usually knew a little about fighting or standing her ground.

"I told Dee I would return her dishes," Cleo said, entering the room and closing the door. "It was very thoughtful of her to bring you a meal."

"I've been the source for a number of stories she's written. I hope this latest one doesn't get back to my boss."

"You should have taken some help."

"Your Uncle Joe said the two men claimed to be bounty hunters. I had no reason to think they were anything else."

Skepticism showed in her makeup, but she let the matter pass. "Do you need anything? We don't have a real doctor in town, but if you—"

He waved a hand to discharge the notion. "I'm all right. Just a bruise here or there. I'll be stiff for a day or two, but I've taken a few thumpings before."

"How about some more water or a fresh towel so you can clean up?" she asked. "Do you have a change of clothes?"

"I've been getting everything laundered every day or two," he informed her. "You don't have to fuss over me."

"I am not given to fussing over a man," she retorted.

Wes wondered at the strained tone of voice. "I was trying to be tactful, while being appreciative of your concern," he said.

"I understand," she said, picking up the tray and starting to leave.

"You and Dee?" he asked a bit hesitantly. "Uh, did you reach some kind of agreement?"

"Yes," she said, walking to the door. "You could say that."

Wes thought she might elaborate, but she went out

the door and closed it behind her without another word. It left him with a thousand unanswered questions.

"If I live to be a hundred, I don't think I'll ever understand womenfolk," he lamented to the empty room. "No, sir, not ever."

Chapter Twelve

Latigo found the old cabin and had a fire going before full dark. Emmett put up the horses, rounded up enough firewood for the night, and entered as Latigo emptied an airtight of beans into a pan.

"Handy, you knowing about this place, Latigo."

"I could lead you to a thousand places to spend the night," Latigo said in reply. "I've spent many a night in caves, hollows, abandoned shacks, and old mines. I can't count the number of times I've done cut wood for a meal at a ranch or farm. And if there's a poker game going within a hundred miles around, I can find it."

"You must really enjoy the game."

"It passes the time and occupies the mind, son. Over the years, I've had a lot of time to occupy." As he spoke, Latigo placed the pan over the flames. A previous occupant, probably the man who built the cabin, had placed two rocks in a position for supporting a kettle, pot, or frying pan. Then Latigo added a little sorghum syrup and a couple of pieces of salt pork. As the concoction began to heat, he added some spices.

"You carry a fair amount of stuff for cooking."

"I've been on my own for the past fifteen years. A man learns to carry the necessities with him."

"You never wanted to settle down and have a family?"

"I tried that once," Latigo admitted seriously. "It didn't work out." Before Emmett could follow up on the statement, he turned the subject toward him.

"What about you? I hear tell you've tossed your loop after that little fireball who writes for the newspaper."

Emmett's face softened at the mention of her. "Yeah. I don't know where it will lead, but I'm giving her my best shot."

"She grilled me like a steak on a spit, trying to get a story," Latigo said. "There's a gal with a lot of ambition. You know, that can get in the way of courtship, especially if the gal and guy have different goals."

"She wants to be a reporter for a big newspaper." His mood became glum. "I'm right certain the career means more to her than me."

"That's a tough bronco to bust, my friend," Latigo said. "It's hard enough to make a life together when you both want the same thing. I know." He swallowed the rise of regret that rose to infiltrate his speech. "Even when you both start out going in the same direction, it doesn't mean it will work out. There are crossroads in every life. Sometimes the woman wants to go one way and the man the other. I thought my wife and I were both after the same thing, yet I ended up on my own for fifteen years and left my wife alone to raise our son."

"I'm sorry," Emmett said softly. "I didn't know."

"It was my fault. I took some risks that didn't pan out. Next thing I'm watching my family starve. I did the only thing I could think of, even though I knew at the time it was wrong. It was a coward's way out." He heaved a breath. "Took a dedicated hound dog like Marshal Gavin to finally track me down, but in truth, I've been a prisoner to my past all these years."

"Now you're working with the marshal to help save a man from going to prison. I'd say you're making a start to balance the books."

He paused to turn the pork strips and stir the beans before commenting. "I'm doing what I can, but there's no way for me to give my wife back those long and lonely years. She died a few years back, and I haven't been able to speak to my son about it. I know he hates me for the way I deserted them. I don't blame him one bit, but I sure wish I could make it up to him."

"Life doesn't always work out the way we want, Latigo. Even your best horse might one day break its leg. All you can do is put the critter out of its misery and move on. No one can turn back the hands of time; what's done is done."

"I reckon you're right, son, but it sure don't stop a man from wishing he could back up a few steps and make things right."

"You've made a start in the right direction by searching for this gambler, and it's all for the sake of Glen Van Ness."

Latigo grinned. "You're right, my young friend. This will be my first step to redemption, and that's the gospel truth."

The sun had brightened the world outside by the time Wes eased out of bed. Had his window faced east instead of west, he would have been awakened much earlier. He was stiff and felt a dozen tender spots where he had been kicked or hit. With his shirt off, he began to inspect several bruises.

The door suddenly pushed open, and Cleo stood with a tray in her hand. She blinked in surprise at seeing him standing there, catching Wes bare-chested for the second time.

"A proper lady ought to learn to knock," Wes teased her.

A pink hue rushed to color her cheeks, but she turned her chagrin against him. "Don't you ever wear a shirt?"

"It's not my first priority when I'm shaving and washing up."

She entered, pausing to kick the door closed with the heel of her foot. "I didn't think you would be up and about for a day or two."

"Nice of you to bring me breakfast, Miss Van Ness. You fussing over me could give me the idea you are taken with me."

"You're helping my brother," she countered. "I would do the same if it were Latigo who had gotten beaten like a dirty rug."

Wes took a moment to gingerly ease into his shirt. Buttoning the shirtfront, he grinned. "I find it difficult to believe that you would have kissed Latigo."

She stepped over and placed the tray on a table next to the bed. "Yes, well, I am not proud of what I did. It was more to strike back at Dee than . . . than to . . . to . . ."

Wes moved over to stand next to her. "Yes?" he prodded, again enjoying her discomfort.

"I'm not like that," she said haughtily. "I don't go around kissing men."

"I should hope not."

"Besides, it's not like you asked me to kiss you. I mean . . . you hadn't tried to . . ." Another flustered pause.

"I know how you feel. After all, we hardly know each other." Wes offered up a flirtatious grin. "If it would help to soothe your conscience, I've never had a better kiss."

"That's not what I'm talking about."

"Oh, you mean reciprocation?"

"And what is that?" She put her hands on her hips and met him squarely. "Reciprocation?"

Wes took her into his arms and showed her. He kissed her before she could muster forth any resistance. It didn't quite turn out as he had hoped. She let him linger about two seconds before she drove a doubled fist into his ribs. It was not a hard blow, but she happened to hit his bruised side. He not only let go, he collapsed downward toward the floor from the intense jolt that raked his entire body.

He would have gone to his knees, but the girl quickly wrapped both of her arms around him. Then she guided him around to his bed and let him sag down. She released him at once, but regret shone brightly on her face.

"You said you were all right!" she scolded him.

Folded at the middle, Wes had to take several short breaths before the spasms of agony subsided and he was able to sit up straight.

"I may not be"—he had to take another short breath—"quite 100 percent just yet," he finished.

Cleo had a pained expression on her face. She turned and sat down in the chair next to his bed. "You'd better stay in bed and try to recover your strength today. If one little poke puts you on the floor, you won't be much help in any kind of a fight."

Wes bobbed his head up and down in agreement, slowly relaxing back to a supine position. Once he could breathe normally, he apologized. "I had no right to do that, Miss Van Ness. I'm usually a perfect gentleman around a lady. Kissing you was poor judgment and rude. I'm sorry."

"Serves me right for not knowing what *reciprocation* means."

"No, it isn't your fault. I don't know you well enough to hold your hand, let alone kiss you. We've only shared a few hours together. A man and a woman ought to get to know each other for a good long time before they get romantic."

"Is that what you call it—romantic?" She harrumphed at the notion. "You took advantage of me."

"No more than you did when you kissed me," he reminded her.

"I explained about that. It was to get back at Dee."

"And I was squaring up the ante between us, so you didn't have to feel like you owed me something. You know, you kissed me, I kissed you—now we're even. Isn't that fair?"

Her shoulders drooped. "I'm not sure what is fair when it comes to courting, Mr. Gavin. You're only the second man I ever kissed, and I hardly know you. I . . . it makes me feel like a floozy."

"If it will put your mind at ease, I've spoken to nearly everyone in town about you," Wes admitted. "They all say the same thing—Cleo Van Ness is the nicest girl in the country. I'm the one not worthy of the affection and caring you've shown me."

She immediately came to his defense. "You're a deputy U.S. marshal. You're trying to help clear my brother of a murder charge. And you risk your life for all of us, keeping the peace and going after murderers and bandits. I'd say that ought to count for something."

He regarded her with a serious scrutiny. "If you can overlook my impulsive behavior just now, I'll not hold your first kiss against you."

"That's fair."

"And if I might be so bold, I'd admire to court you properly, Miss Van Ness."

A slight smile came to play on her lips. "When you are back on your feet, I would like that very much, Mr. Gavin."

Cleo told Shep not to expect Wes for another day. Then she spoke to Glen and found he was a bit more optimistic.

"That old gent Latigo said he was pretty sure he could find Duke's pal."

"Mr. Gavin seems to believe he can do it as well. He had Shep wire Denver and tell them not to bother with a circuit judge. He had already told his office to hold off sending the prison wagon until your case was settled."

Glen showed a genuine concern. "The man is risking his neck sitting here with these Quinteen boys. They've been talking about how their pa will have the whole gang rounded up in no time. They claim their kin will burn down the town and kill everyone in it, if Gavin don't let them loose."

"There's no chance of him letting them go," Cleo told him. "Wes Gavin isn't a man to turn his back on the law."

"I'm responsible for all this trouble. The marshal is sticking here because of me. If I had just given Duke a beating, I wouldn't be in here, and these two Quinteens would be in Denver by now."

"What is it Daddy says about regret?"

Glen groaned. "Yeah, I know. He has a saying for everything. The one you're talking about is about doing it right the first time, because 'you can't turn back the clock and do something over.' "

"I'm staying in town today. If you'd like, I'll bring you supper."

"Shep has been feeding us pretty good. Usually whatever special Bertha is having over at her Eatery," he said. "Did you see what she had written down on her menu board for tonight?"

"Meat loaf."

Glen uttered another groan. "I'd better have you get

my supper. I hear the last time she threw out meat loaf leftovers, three dogs left town."

Cleo laughed. Glen smiled the way he used to, back when he was carefree and fun to be around. During the years Matt was alive, Glen had lived a happy-go-lucky existence. This was the first time she had seen him relax since being put in jail.

"I'll get you the same thing I pick up for Mr. Gavin."

"He going to be all right?"

"I'm forcing him to rest up today, but I'm sure he'll be up and around by tomorrow." She winked. "He's like you, tougher than coiled wire."

"I can tell when you talk about him that you like the guy." It was a statement.

"We are in the process of getting acquainted, but yes, I do like him."

Glen warned her, "You know a marshal like him has the life of a drifter, chasing all over the country after outlaws."

"I think he would settle down for the right woman."

He chuckled and displayed a mischievous smirk. "I see trouble on the horizon for our marshal, and it has nothing to do with the Quinteens."

Chapter Thirteen

The gambler at the poker table said his name was Joe Clegg, but Latigo didn't believe him. He saw him do a little cheating, but the man was careful, trying to win with the cards dealt and betting mostly on good hands. He had bluffed on at least three occasions and lost twice, both times to Latigo.

While hiding from the law over the years, Latigo had played cards to pass his endless days and nights. Gaining a measure of skill at the tables, he often went months before a streak of bad luck forced him to seek out another quarry and renew his stake. He knew how to palm a card, slip the bottom card, or cut himself to a high card. There were many tricks the crooked gamblers used, and he had seen and mastered most of them. However, he seldom cheated when playing, except to best a cardsharp. It was an absurdity that he would rob a man at gunpoint but not cheat at poker. But that was partly the reason for him robbing so many slippery-fingered gamblers—to teach them a lesson for being dishonest.

Latigo sat at the table for several hours, while Emmett wandered around bored and waited for his signal. They had ridden into Lost Gulch separately and had not spoken or acknowledged they knew each other. It was necessary to keep Emmett at a safe distance so he could do his job without causing undue attention.

It was after midnight when the game began to break up. Latigo was a few dollars up, but everyone else had lost money except for the man calling himself Joe. When two of the players left the table, Latigo took a moment to yawn and stretch.

"Been a full day, fellows," he said to the two remaining at the table. "One more hand and I'm calling it a night."

The man to his right, a local rancher named Carson, pushed the pile of cards his way. "Your deal, old-timer. How about a good hand? I ain't won squat all night."

"Coming right up," Latigo said, tossing out his ante. "You are about due."

Before Latigo began, he checked and saw that Emmett had picked up his signal. Scooping up the deck and loose cards, he shuffled several times and placed the deck on the table and let the rancher cut.

Timing Emmett's approach, he picked up the deck at the moment Emmett suddenly stumbled and bumped into the table, causing an empty glass to tip over and both men to look up at him.

"Uh, sorry, fellas," he muttered, staggering a bit uncertainly for the barroom counter.

Latigo had used the minute's interruption to scoot his chair back, as if to keep from being knocked over. The movement covered the lowering of his hand and quick exchange of the deck for one he had prepared and had ready on his lap. Placing the stacked deck on the table, he used a hand to pull his chair closer and tucked away the original deck of cards at the same time.

"Good thing this is the last hand," he said, beginning to deal. "The drunks are about the only ones left in the casino."

He dealt the cards and sat back, watching both players with his peripheral vision while appearing to study his own hand. Joe opened with twenty dollars; the rancher matched the twenty and raised twenty more. Latigo folded.

"What kind of gambler are you, folding on the last hand?" Carson teased.

"The kind who doesn't think he can get a decent hand when having to draw five cards."

Carson laughed, and Joe met and upped his raise.

Latigo watched patiently until there was over a hundred dollars in the pot. Then Joe, who he knew had three queens, called the final raise and asked for two cards. The rancher, who had been given three aces, also tossed away two cards. Latigo sent each man the cards he had prepared ahead of time and waited.

Both men raised the pot until the rancher had put everything he had left into the middle. Joe displayed a cruel sneer and raised him the hundred and six dollars he still had in front of him.

"I can't call your bet," the rancher groaned. "Everything I've got is already in the pot."

Latigo shrugged. "I take you for an honest man, Carson. I'll lend you the money against your horse and tack." He glanced over at Joe. "Any objections?"

"Put in your chips," he said smugly. "I'm feeling lucky."

"Luck has been with you tonight," Latigo admitted, while pushing a fair portion of his own chips into the middle of the table. "But she can be a fickle mistress sometimes."

Joe laughed. "Not this time, old-timer." He spread out his cards to show four queens. "This time she's right there on the table!"

But Carson smiled in triumph and laid his own cards out for Joe to see. "First time I've had four aces dealt to me in fifteen years. Couldn't have come at a better time."

Joe's jaw about hit the tabletop. His eyes bugged out in shock as Carson raked in his winnings. His face worked, his hand went down to his pocket, and he started to rise up from his chair. He might have pulled a gun, but Emmett had slipped over to watch the final hand and was at his back. He placed a firm hand on the man's shoulder, forcing him to remain seated, while his own gun pressed against the back of his head.

"Slow and easy, mister," he warned. "Let's see what you're reaching for in your pocket."

Carson started to question what was going on, but Latigo waved him to silence. He leaned over the table and put a hard look on the gambler.

"You're Yancy Pine," he said. "I remember you. You're the guy who used to work tables with that crooked cardsharp, the one who called himself Duke."

"I've seen you before too," Emmett said, backing up

the lie. "You like to walk behind the players when the game is on, then signal to your partner so he knows how to bid." He displayed a mirthless smile. "I believe you've also wandered into a table a time or two, the way I did tonight, so Duke could switch cards."

"That's what I did when my friend hit our table," Latigo admitted. "I stacked a deck of matching cards for three players. I wanted to wait until the place was clearing out, in case you were a little too quick with your hideaway gun."

He lifted the gun up using only two fingers and placed it on the table. "I ain't been cheating," he said.

"Yes, you have—spotted at least four times," Latigo said. "So now you have a choice to make. Either we drag you out, hang you by the heels, and tar and feather you, or you can take a ride with me and my friend."

The man nervously licked his lips. "Ride? Ride where?"

"Back to Sunset, where you can tell the sheriff how you removed Duke's gun after he was killed trying to shoot it out with a man outside one of the saloons."

"I don't understand," Carson said, finally speaking up. "You stacked the deck so I would win?"

"Because I don't know you, it was easier for me to have you win than take the chance someone would think I was cheating. Yancy here did cheat several times, so you can take the pot, except for the money you borrowed from me."

Carson counted out the money and cleared the table. He stood up and put a murderous look on Yancy, as Latigo was putting his own money into his pocket. "You best ride with these men, while you're still able to sit a saddle, mister. I catch you back here, and me and my men will string you up from the nearest tree."

Yancy didn't reply, waiting until Carson had left before he turned back to Latigo. "What makes you think I'll say what you want when I reach Sunset?"

"You only have to tell the truth."

The man set his teeth. "Duke and me worked together for ten years. We were as close as brothers."

"You shouldn't have gone to Sunset. Glen Van Ness said he had warned you both to stay out of town. He knew you two had cheated him the last time."

"He was guessing about that. Duke took most of his money without any help from me."

"Still, he tried to pull a gun on the boy. Pretty stupid to do something like that when you're on the ground and a guy is standing over you ready to shoot."

Yancy didn't reply to that, so Emmett shoved the gun against his neck a second time. "We could always say this weasel admitted the truth about Duke having a gun, and then let Carson take care of him. I reckon the other two guys from the table would be interested in how come they managed to lose their money tonight."

"Hold on a minute." Yancy was suddenly more agreeable. "I took the gun so everyone would think that the Van Ness kid shot Duke in cold blood, but it wasn't so he would end up in jail or with a noose around his neck."

"Then why?" Latigo asked.

"So people around Sunset would have nothing but contempt for him, that's why! His uncle is the judge, and his pa thinks he owns the town. The kid himself never did one damned thing to earn the position of top dog.

Far as I know, the only thing he ever did was drink and gamble and chase after women. After he loses a few bucks at the table, he tells us to tuck our tails and git!" Yancy snorted. "I didn't agree with Duke when he wanted to go back there, but it rankled me too, being told to grab my pants and run."

"Well, it just so happens the folks in Sunset are not as meek around the Van Ness family as you thought. They put Glen in jail and wired to have a circuit judge hear his case." Latigo let the information sink in before continuing. "There was a witness to the shooting, but she didn't see you take Duke's gun. I know that boy has learned a lesson by being locked up, but he sure doesn't deserve to end up doing twenty years behind bars or maybe being hanged."

Yancy regarded Latigo with a steady gaze. Finally, he let out a breath and bobbed his head. "All right, I'll go with you and tell it straight. I never figured Glen would get any jail time, not with him being a Van Ness. Guess there's more justice at Sunset than I thought."

"You won't mind if we keep you company tonight," Emmett said. "It would trouble us greatly if you were to have a change of heart during the night and slip away."

"I've got a room with two beds at the rooming house. So long as I get one bed, I don't care if you two figure a way to share the other."

Latigo grinned. "You're a real gentleman, Yancy. Being so kindhearted and all, I'll share my winnings with you so you don't ride away without a poke from Sunset."

"You two boys are all heart."

Emmett curled his lips into a sneer. "It's better than being tarred and feathered—wouldn't you say?"

"Yeah, whatever you say," Yancy admitted, but his voice lacked any enthusiasm.

Cleo was walking over to Bertha's Eatery when Dee came out of the newspaper office. She had an armload of newspapers, obviously taking her daily delivery to the general store. She paused and waited for Cleo.

"So why am I not surprised you're still in town?" she said as a greeting.

Cleo smiled and offered no comment. "I wanted to let Marshal Gavin sleep in. I'm going to get breakfast for him and my brother at the same time. Kip and Scat are helping Shep tend to the other prisoners."

"When do you get to eat?"

"I'll grab something while I'm there."

"Let me drop these off, and I'll join you," Dee offered. "I've already had breakfast, but I can have a cup of coffee while you eat."

Cleo smiled and walked with her to the store, relieved to have the animosity gone between them. She had some friends, but Dee was the only girl close to her own age and unmarried. They should have been best friends, instead of always fighting and competing.

At Bertha's place, Cleo ordered full meals for Glen and Wes and then added a plate of eggs and toast with honey for herself. It was about the least expensive item on the menu, but she chose it because she wasn't usually hungry for the morning meal.

"I'm like that too," Dee remarked after Cleo had explained her order. "Dad says I have the appetite of a hummingbird—and flitter about as much too."

Cleo laughed. "My father has the habit of asking if I'm feeling all right. He thinks anyone who doesn't eat five pounds of food at a sitting must be ill."

"So," Dee said, turning serious, "tell me what has happened since I let you have Marshal Gavin all to yourself."

Cleo tried to hide the heat of embarrassment by ducking her head, but Dee was a newshound. She automatically understood far more than anything Cleo was prepared to say.

"I knew it!" she said excitedly. "Something happened! Tell me!"

"Nothing happened . . . exactly." She tried to calm her enthusiasm. "I mean, we have talked quite a lot, and I have taken him his meals. He will be back to working today."

Dee pleaded, "Come on, Cleo—give! I allowed you to have the man all to yourself. I know you're holding out on me."

"Well, there was one thing." At Dee's expectant look, she sighed and confessed, "Wes reciprocated me."

The news caused Dee to pause, and then her face scrunched into a puzzled frown. "He *reciprocated* you?" she asked.

Cleo wondered if Wes had made up the word. "Yes, he said he had to reciprocate so we would be even."

"Oh!" Dee cried, comprehending. "You mean he kissed you!"

Nearly every head in the café turned to look at them. Cleo put a hand over her brow to hide her face and stared at the tabletop.

"Gads, Dee!" she hissed her displeasure. "You don't have to tell the whole world."

But Dee was laughing. "I'm sorry, Cleo," she said between bursts of giggles, "but I never heard of anyone
being *reciprocated* before."

"I knew I shouldn't tell you."

"Of course you should, Cleo. That's what girlfriends
do. They confide in each other."

"Oh, sure, as if you would confide in me about Emmett."

"I've let him kiss me a few times." Dee was instantly
forthcoming. "You might say he's my steady beau at the
moment, the only guy I'm courting."

Cleo risked a quick glance around to see if everyone
was still staring at them, but the diners had returned to
eating and talking among themselves. When she put her
attention back on Dee, she saw something she had never
seen before. Dee was smiling happily back at her. It was
something she had missed, having a real girlfriend—even
if she did happen to have a big, loud mouth.

"So what's your strategy, girl?" Dee asked. "How are
you going to corral that fine stallion?"

"I have no idea," she said, munching on a piece of
toast.

"Maybe we ought to put our heads together and think
up a plan. I've got all the time in the world to snare
Emmett, but you might only have a few days to work on
Wes. We have to figure a way to get you two together."

"I was going to go back to the ranch today," she said,
taking another bite from her breakfast.

"Not by a jugful, you're not. In the words of my father,
we've got to work on that man until he is 'tetotaciously
exflunctified.'"

Cleo about choked on a mouthful of toast. "Do—do what?" she sputtered.

Dee waved a hand. "My father can be highfalutin and verbose at times. He is like a walking dictionary, and I'm pretty sure he makes up words himself sometimes."

"So what does it mean?"

"It means we have to make sure you win the marshal's heart in the short time we have."

Cleo decided she was not going to eat any more of the food on the plate. Instead, she regarded her new friend with a narrowed-eyed suspicion. "I can see now why I never got the best of you."

Dee snickered. "The best is what I've saved for working *with* you!" She put a coin on the table for her coffee. "Come on."

"But the food for Glen and the marshal?"

"We'll tell Bertha to set it aside until we get back."

Chapter Fourteen

Sentry arose from his bed on the ground and walked over to stand next to Hyrum. The leader of the gang didn't look at him but continued to stare down the trail. "They ought to be back today," he said softly to Hyrum. "We're near out of everything to eat, and we're having to reuse the old grounds for coffee."

Hyrum finally glanced over at him and then checked to see the others were out of earshot. "I'm concerned about this delay. If that marshal gets it in his head that we might be close by, he will have time to set up a reception for us."

"He didn't tag us for riding with you," Sentry assured him. "He had seen one of those old dodgers on Rojas and me, from our days of working alone. No way he could know we were scouting out the town to find out where Lark's boys were at."

"This help you spoke of—any idea how many men are backing the marshal?"

"Far as we know, only the hometown sheriff. The

man who stepped in to stop us from killing Gavin might have only been a good Samaritan."

"We best figure he has at least one or two more. And what about the guy he met up with before he captured Buster and Butch?"

"The barkeep said an older gent came in with the marshal, but he didn't know much about him. Said him and Shep, the local lawman, were the ones watching the jail, but the older guy left town."

"Left town?"

"So the bartender said."

"Think they were working together, and now the one has left for some reason?"

"I don't know. From the trail we followed back into that box canyon, it appeared the marshal was following that jasper, right up until the man's horse came up lame. Nothing about the business between those two makes sense."

"Well, it won't matter if he's left town. It's one less man to worry about."

"Hope your boys get here pretty soon," Sentry said, after they had been silent a short while. "I'm anxious to put this behind us and get back to work." He paused to finger his swollen face. "And I'm going to watch for that big fellow on the street when we ride in. I owe him a little payback."

"My boys will be back today," Hyrum promised. "We'll decide when to go into town once they arrive."

Sentry sighed. "Can't be soon enough to suit me."

"Too bad they don't have a bank in Sunset. We could pick up a little coin while we're getting the boys out of jail."

"Might be a little cash at one of the two saloons, but that would mean taking on the whole town."

"Too many ways to get one of us killed trying to pull something like that. Once we have the gang back together, we'll head for Leadville. There are payrolls running up into the mining town all the time. We'll pick us a ripe plum to pluck."

"Sounds good to me, Hyrum. Rojas and I are ready to start earning some money."

Wes had been up for an hour, had washed and shaved, and even had his boots on. He was expecting Cleo to bring him breakfast, as she had told him she would do that one final chore before she allowed him to go back to work. This time he was prepared for her visit, or so he thought.

When the light tap came at the door, he pulled it open and was ready with his greeting. "I was beginning to think you might have left," he began, stepping back to allow her to enter. When he saw her, the words died in his throat, and he gawked stupidly.

Cleo held a tray with a plate of food on it, but it wasn't the breakfast that caused his mental lapse. The girl's golden-blond hair was down about her shoulders, other than the neat row of bangs that decorated her forehead. Brushed to a healthy sheen, it set off her face like a fabulous, ornate frame encasing an exquisite portrait. A closer inspection showed a hint of rouge on her lips and cheeks. The dress was even more stunning than the one she had worn to the dance, light blue with white lace and trim, and snug enough to accentuate her mature figure. His foolish gaping caused a demure smile to play on her lips.

"Whoa!" Wes breathed the word.

Cleo's trim eyebrows drew together slightly. "What is that supposed to mean?"

Wes unscrambled his brain and swallowed his amazement. "I reckon it just slipped out. I don't have the fancy words to tell you how beautiful you are."

"Are looks so important?"

"I reckon beauty means something different to most everyone. For a cattleman, it might be his calves, a farmer maybe sees it in his crops sprouting, while a woman watches her baby take his first step." He took a step closer and met her gaze steadily. "The beauty I see in you comes from more than a fine dress and the glistening of your golden hair. When I look into your eyes, I see everything good and special a man could ever hope to find in this world."

Cleo's mouth opened slightly as if she would speak, but then she pursed her lips and stepped past Wes to put the tray on the table next to his bed. When she revolved about, she had an odd look on her face.

"I admit that I feel an . . . attraction for you, Marshal Gavin," she murmured. "But I can't see any future in it."

"Because of my line of work?"

"Yes," she said quietly. "You will soon leave here with your prisoners. And I still don't know how I feel about you."

"So why did you dress up to leave me speechless?"

"My heart keeps trying to tell my head what to do. I listened to my heart—and Dee's advice—before I came here this morning. But I won't allow myself to fall in love with a man who is gone off after killers or bandits for weeks at a time. I wouldn't want to sit home alone and wonder if you are lying out on the prairie wounded or dead. I couldn't accept a life like that."

"My father was a foreman for a fair-sized ranch, so I know a little about cattle. If I had a good reason, I would find something else to do that would allow me to work mostly regular hours and be home every night."

"You would do that for a woman?"

Wes moved over next to Cleo and placed his hands on her shoulders. He was drawn to the warmth in her gaze and smiled.

"I'd sure enough do it for the *right* woman."

Cleo didn't throw herself into his arms and kiss him. Instead, she leaned forward until she could place her head against his shoulder. He engulfed her within his arms, and they remained that way, in a tender embrace, a sharing of their feelings without expressing words.

Wes gently kneaded her back with the tips of his fingers, feeling that this was the woman he was meant to share his life with. And it was amazing.

Latigo topped the ridge first and pulled his mount to a stop. He raised a hand to keep Emmett and Yancy from speaking.

"There's a group of riders coming yonder," he whispered to them. "Over there, coming up the valley trail."

"Check out below," Emmett said in a hushed voice. "Looks like a camp with several men. I'll bet it's the Quinteens."

Silently, Latigo urged them back over the crest of the hill, where they were out of sight of both groups of men.

He pondered ideas as he searched the hills for a route that would take them around the men below.

"What do you think?" Emmett asked.

"We need to go around those fellows," he replied. "We wouldn't want them spotting us; they might decide to keep us from reaching Sunset."

"We can cut through the hills and pick up the main road a half mile east of here," Emmett suggested. "You think those men belong to the Quinteen gang?"

"Be my guess," Latigo said.

"They're putting together a small army."

Latigo was turning ideas over in his head. If something wasn't done, the Quinteen gang would be riding into town with at least nine or ten men. A lot of people could get killed in a raid like that. His boy, Shep; the marshal; and a good many townspeople would all be in danger. That couldn't be allowed to happen. If only there was a way to take the fight somewhere else and move the battle away from town. But how did a man control where and when a gang of murderers might attack?

"I've an idea in mind," he said after a few long moments. With a glance at the sky, Latigo turned to the other two men. "It'll be dark in a few hours, and it will take time for those men to get organized. Let's head to town and let the marshal know the Quinteen gang is on the town's doorstep."

Emmett did not hide his worry. "I counted five riders coming, and there are four or five down in the camp. It's going to take a lot of firepower to match that many guns."

"Can't worry about that now. We need to straighten out Glen's problem first so he isn't in the way of whatever happens. Me and the marshal will worry about the gang."

Emmett frowned. "I know Gavin is a deputy U.S. marshal, but even he is no match for near a dozen men."

"First, we'll clear up Glen's case. Then we'll discuss how to handle the Quinteen gang."

Latigo led the way, exiting from the main trail so they could make their way up a nearby ravine. There were several deer and animal trails, not to mention a number of cattle grazing in the area, so they were able to move without making a lot of noise. As the three of them threaded around the brush and ducked an occasional tree branch, Latigo mulled over his idea and sorted out a few details. With luck, he might yet prove himself worthy of being called a father again.

Once the three men arrived in town, Dee and Judge Stevens were summoned to listen to Yancy tell his story. Kip, Scat, and Pepper also crowded into the small office. Yancy gave a full account of Duke's actions and admitted to having removed his small-caliber gun. When he finished, he said, "Latigo promised I could ride out after I told the truth."

Wes looked at the judge. When the man gave an affirmative nod, he said, "You're free to go, Yancy. Just don't get your name on any more dodgers."

"Duke was the one with the temper," he claimed. "He got us in trouble with the law when he shot that banker's son. I've never had any problems with the law myself."

"I'll see that the wanted handbills are removed from active files," Judge Stevens said.

Yancy thanked him and turned to go, but Latigo took hold of the man's arm to stop him. "Best head east out of town. You won't run into any trouble that way."

"I'm in no hurry to meet up with the fellows we saw on our way here," he said. "Think it's about time I headed for Kansas to try my luck at the tables."

As he left the office, the judge declared Glen a free man. Dee hurried off to put the story in the paper, and Emmett shook Glen's hand, while his three friends pounded him on the back.

Glen waved off the congratulations long enough to step over and shake hands with Latigo, Shep, and Wes. He had a serious look on his face.

"You done good by me, all of you," he said. "Anything you need, you've only got to ask."

Wes took advantage of the offer. "I'd appreciate one or two of your pals sticking around to help guard the jail. Shep has a store to run, and I'm not up to working around the clock just yet."

"I'll stay," Kip volunteered.

"Me too," Scat vowed. "Long as you need us, Marshal, you only got to say the word."

Glen laughed. "Looks like you didn't have to ask me for help at all."

"I'm glad this worked out for you."

Emmett put his hands on his hips and regarded Latigo with a hard stare. "About time you spoke up, Lat."

All eyes went to the Gentleman Bandit. He hesitated only long enough to glance shamefully at his son. "The Quinteen gang is a half mile outside of town."

The quiet in the room was broken at once by Buster

and Butch. "Told you!" cried one of them. "Your time is up, Marshal!" shouted the other. "We'll soon be dancing all over your dead body."

Scat took a step toward them, pointed a warning finger at the two men, and they fell silent at once.

Lat spoke in a lowered voice. "Now, I've come up with a plan, Marshal, and I think you ought to give a listen."

"What kind of plan?" Wes asked.

"A way to keep the gang out of Sunset. They come riding in here, and there will be a lot of shooting. They might even set fire to the town. My idea will keep Shep and everyone else out of harm's way and give us a chance to eliminate the Quinteen gang once and for all—but we'll need some help."

"You can count me in," Glen said.

"Us too," Kip vowed.

"Every man jack at the ranch will help if needed," Emmett told him.

Wes looked at Shep. The young man gave a solemn nod. "I'm willing to hear what Latigo has to say."

"Tell us your idea," Wes said.

Latigo slipped over to the livery as the sun touched the distant horizon. He had bat-sized butterflies flapping about in his chest, but there was also a feeling of satisfaction. He was going to do something necessary, something that would save lives. Wes had allowed that his plan was worth trying. All he needed to do was convince the Quinteens—without getting himself killed in the process.

A man stepped out with the reins of Gavin's horse. It wasn't the liveryman, Joe Fremont. It was Shep.

"I know why you picked me to stay behind," he said. "You want to protect me."

"You're a family man, you have a store to run, and you're the telegraph operator," Latigo said. "It's logical that you stay behind."

"Unless the Quinteens guess your plan."

"We don't want a fight in town, Shep. Too many people could get hurt."

"What about you?" he asked. "You're sticking your neck out a long way to make this plan work."

"It's my plan."

"You wouldn't be trying to make up for all the time you should have been taking care of Mom and me?"

Latigo's chin fell, and he sighed, "I can't undo all the years of neglect—I know that. I should have stayed there with you and kept trying until I found some way to keep our family together."

"Instead you robbed someone and sent us money."

"Yes, the first man I ever robbed was the only one who didn't deserve it," Latigo admitted. "However, I left payment on his doorstep with interest a few months later. After him, I targeted people who had taken advantage of people or cheated them. I'm not saying that makes my crimes any better, but I never took money from another innocent person." He sighed. "There is nothing moral about stealing, even when the money is used for something good. I done the deeds, and I deserve to go to jail for it. That's why I stuck with Marshal Gavin. He's the kind of man I wish I could have been, honest as the day is long and willing to risk his life sticking here to see that Glen got a fair hearing."

Shep agreed on that point. "He sure saved me from shooting Kip or one of his pals when he first arrived— maybe saved me from getting shot too."

"That's why I've got to do this," Latigo told Shep. "I'm through walking away from my responsibilities."

"I can't forgive you for not being there for Mom and me all those years."

"No, and I don't expect you to. I wish I had done things different, but I can't change the past. However, I'd sure like to be friends with you from here on. And I dearly love your kids and wife."

"I can't forget who you were. It's too much to ask."

Latigo nodded his understanding. "I don't expect you to forget, son. I wanted to get to know you before I told you the truth. I can only ask you not to think of me as the man I was, but the man I am now. And I don't have a lot of time, because I've got to get to the Quinteen camp before they decide to make their raid tonight."

Shep met his look with a hard scrutiny. After a moment, he relaxed ever so slightly and stuck out his hand.

"I wish you luck, Latigo."

Shaking the hand, Latigo felt the sting of tears in his eyes, and a lump of emotion blocked the forming of any words. He turned quickly and mounted his horse.

Chapter Fifteen

Dee was there when Emmett came from the meeting. She smiled, and his heart began to soar. It wasn't fair that a simple expression of greeting could lift his feet off the ground.

"You get the story finished already?" he asked.

"Dad is setting the print right now. Mother is taking a copy over to have Shep send it by wire to Denver. The news about Glen's innocence will be secondary if the marshal manages to get the Quinteen boys to trial."

"About that, we've got a plan to keep the gang from shooting up the town."

"What do you mean, 'we've got a plan'?"

"I'm on my way to the ranch. Glen is sticking here with Kip, Scat, and Pepper, in case the gang attacks to-night. You and your folks will want to stay off the street and keep your door locked."

"What?" Dee was shocked. "What are you saying, Emmett? Why would the Quinteens come tonight?"

"You left before we discussed it," he told her. "The

gang is outside of town about a half mile or so down the road. We had to go around them when we came in with Yancy."

"So what's going on?"

He explained the plan to her quickly and finished with, "That's why I'm riding to the ranch. If they hit the town, I'll need every man I can get to ride in and drive them off."

"You're going to be in the middle of a gunfight?" she queried, her face displaying some anxiety at the idea. "You are risking your life?"

"They are a band of thieves and killers, Dee. Me and some of the boys will keep watch over the town tonight."

"But if they come, you might be killed!"

"I'm taking no more chances than Marshal Gavin, and less than Latigo, because he's the one who is going to their camp."

"Latigo is going to ride into the Quinteen encampment? What if they kill him?"

Emmett couldn't answer that. "He was the one who came up with the idea, so he is the one taking the risk."

"And you? How much risk are you taking?"

"I'll do my best not to get myself killed, if that's what worries you."

Dee suddenly moved forward, putting her arms around his waist. Her eyes misted, and she gazed up at him with a look he had never seen on her face before.

"I'm afraid for you, Emmett. I . . . it's strange, but I never thought about losing you."

He was surprised by her confession. "You've continually put me off and said we shouldn't get too serious."

The girl gave a shake of her head. "I didn't think about . . . I mean, I didn't know I cared as much as I do. The thought of you being hurt or killed . . ." Her voice was lost to a gulp of emotion.

The declaration was the most beautiful music Emmett had ever heard. "What about you leaving Sunset?" he asked. "You said you might get a job in Denver after having all your latest stories written in the newspaper there."

"So?" She didn't deny the notion. "You're a man of many talents. You could find work there, and probably for a lot more money than Mr. Van Ness pays you."

Emmett was stunned. "You mean that you would want me to go with you?"

"I won't make the best wife, chasing after stories all the time. You're liable to end up doing much of the cooking. And you'll have to work in a bank or a store, something that allows us to have our evenings and Sundays together. It'll take a lot of sacrifice on your part, but I want to one day be an editor and write books too."

Emmett leaned down and kissed her lightly on the lips. "I'm not crazy about working out in the weather all the time, playing nursemaid to a bunch of cows. I reckon I could find work at a business or even start up one of my own. I'm pretty handy with leather goods, and I've made saddles for Cleo and several of the guys out at the ranch."

"Emmett, are you asking me to marry you and let you take me away to Denver?"

He laughed at the unique proposal. "I suppose so, providing you can get the job at the newspaper."

Dee kissed him with feeling this time. Then she backed away and put a stern look on her face. "Don't you let anything happen to you tomorrow, Emmett Dodge, or I'll never speak to you again!"

He mounted the horse and smiled down at her. "Whatever you say, Delight Johnson." Emmett felt he could fly but chose to swing the animal around and headed for the ranch on horseback.

Latigo pretended to be looking around when he spied a lookout. The man watching would think he had been forced to search for the camp. He neck-reined his horse in that direction, moving swiftly over to confront the group of men.

Several men put their hands to their guns, although no one pointed one at him. When he stopped his horse, a shaggy, red-haired man came forward. He had gray above his ears, and a bushy rust color in his eyebrows and in the stubble of his beard.

"I'd wager you're Hyrum Quinteen," Latigo spouted excitedly. "Am I glad I found you boys!"

Suspicion flooded the man's features, and his flinty eyes searched the trail in back of Latigo as if looking for other riders.

"What do you want?"

"Name's Latigo Dykes," he explained quickly. "Your boys are locked up in the jail at Sunset. They've been telling me you were coming ever since the three of us ended up as prisoners."

"What are you talking about?"

"The marshal who grabbed your boys also grabbed

me. I'm only a petty thief, so he has let me run errands and the like for him." He chortled. "Fool even let me have a shotgun one time, but only when there were other law dogs around."

"You best tell us why you're here," another older gent said. "Them are my boys in that there jail."

"Okay, okay, I'm getting to it." Latigo looked around. "This all the men you have, only nine of you?"

Hyrum glanced about at his men and then glared at Latigo. "We've enough to get the job done."

"Not if you try and hit the town, you don't. A rider spotted you a few hours ago and alerted the town. As we speak, every man jack in Sunset is posted where they can cover the street. Then there's a half dozen or so men who came in for a local boy's hearing. The marshal got Glen Van Ness released from a murder charge, so he and his pals are looking out for the marshal tonight too."

"What the hell?" Mort said. "We didn't agree to take on twenty or thirty guns. They'll cut us down like weeds in a garden!"

Hyrum waved him to silence and peered up at Latigo. "Why'd you come out here, Dykes?"

"The marshal trusts me—that's how I was able to sneak out of town—but I ain't going to spend the rest of my days breaking rocks at some prison. I've come to tell you a way to get your boys back without a shot being fired."

"And why should we believe anything you have to say?"

Latigo uttered a sigh. "You ever hear of the Gentleman Bandit?" At Hyrum's nod, he hooked a thumb to point at his own chest. "I'm the Gentleman Bandit, and I look to spend ten years behind bars once I reach Denver."

"Makes no sense why the marshal should trust you," Lark said.

Latigo ducked his head as if reluctant to tell the truth. "He has good reason." He heaved a sigh of regret. "Because I saved his life." At their confused expressions, he told them how Buster and Butch had gotten the drop on the marshal and were going to open fire. "But I was on the back of the marshal's horse," he declared. "I'd have been killed along with the lawman if the shooting had started. So I helped to turn the tables on your boys. The marshal took it that I saved his life, but I was only trying to save my own." He gave a sorrowful shake of his head to show his sincerity. "I'm sorry, fellows, but I helped capture those two boys."

Lark snorted his rage. "By thunder! Let's string this no-good louse up from the nearest tree!"

Hyrum restrained him with one arm. "You heard him—he was only saving his own hide."

"You ain't gonna trust him!" Lark barked.

"He's got sand in his craw to come here alone and unarmed," Sentry said.

"Don't sound like hitting the town is such a good idea either," Moab said.

Saul concurred at once. "If we hit the jail, with all those guns in town, half of us would get killed."

Latigo chose that moment to put his plan into motion. "The news is being passed around town that the prison wagon is due in tomorrow. I don't know if you had heard about it or not."

"We figured Gavin wouldn't try to move my nephews on his own," Hyrum replied.

"Yeah, but the rumor is false." Latigo grinned at the old man's surprise. "The marshal was hoping one of your men would overhear the story. That way, you would sit back and wait for the prison wagon. It would be easier to stop the wagon and get your boys back, rather than taking on a town that is heavily fortified against a raid."

"Man's a fox," Sentry said. "Even if the prison wagon did show up, he would probably have hired several more guards."

"Be no less than four guards on that prison wagon to start with," Mort said. "I seen it one time when they grabbed up Butcher Davis, over at Whitewater. Two men on top with shotguns on the wagon and two outriders. They wouldn't be easy pickings even without any extra help."

"There's a safe way to do this," Latigo volunteered. "And you won't have to face the whole town or the prison wagon."

Hyrum eyed him thoughtfully for a short span of time and then asked, "What's this plan of yours?"

By sunup, the covered wagon had been prepared, and the team of horses was put into harness. Wes would drive with Latigo at his side. The idea was to pass themselves off as a couple of teamsters en route to Denver with their freight wagon.

Everything was prepared for transporting the Quinteen boys by the time Emmett returned from the Van

Ness ranch. He didn't arrive alone; Cleo was with him, along with the semi-retired hand, Raul. Cleo wasted no time cornering Wes and moving out of earshot for anyone nearby.

"This is the most dangerous idea I ever heard of!" she sounded off at once. "You and Latigo, riding out in the open like two practice targets to be shot at!"

"It's the best chance we have," he argued. "We don't want the Quinteen gang to hit the jail and maybe kill a dozen people. These people didn't ask for me to come here, so it's my responsibility to keep those killers out of town."

"You're the one who's going to get killed!" Cleo snapped, turning her back on him. "I make a fool of myself over you, and you . . . you . . ."

Wes rested his hands on her shoulders. "This will all work out," he said softly. "You have to trust me."

"I should never have let myself fall in love with you."

He gently rotated her around and drew her close to him. "It'll be all right, little darling," he whispered. "I promise."

She finally lifted her face, allowing him to see the tears in her eyes. "I want to believe you."

"Nothing is more important to me than you," Wes told her truthfully. "I'm doing this because I have to. The Quinteen gang won't stop so long as I have Butch and Buster. This is the only way we can ever be together."

Cleo slipped her arms around him and clung to him tightly. He held her for a few precious seconds before he eased back a step.

"We have to get moving."

"And that murderous gang will swoop down on you and shoot you full of holes."

He smiled at the gloomy statement. "Have a little faith, lady. I'm not some tenderfoot. We'll be just fine."

"You'd better be!" she said with some fire. "I told you before, if you get yourself killed, I won't forgive you—not ever!"

Rather than speak again, he tipped his head down and kissed her.

"You about ready to light out?" Latigo called. "Daylight's burning, sonny boy."

Wes left Cleo standing at the livery. He climbed aboard the wagon and drove over to the jail. He stopped next to the front door long enough to pick up his passengers. Shep was there to watch and wished them well. They both raised a hand in farewell as the wagon rolled out of town.

Sentry came through the trees and rode up to where the rest of the gang had been waiting. He reined up alongside Hyrum and reported to him. "The wagon left a few minutes ago, just the way the Gentleman Bandit said."

"Did you see my boys?" Lark wanted to know.

"I was a hundred yards away, so I couldn't see what shape they were in. But I saw the town sheriff trot them out and load them in the back of the wagon. Soon as they left, the sheriff went over to open his store. He left the door to the sheriff's office wide open."

"He wouldn't leave the door open if he still had prisoners," Lark said.

Hyrum grunted. "Sounds as if the old bandit was telling the truth. There ain't no prison wagon coming. That information was intended to put us off the scent."

"Yep, if we had heard the story being spread around, we'd have been sitting here watching for that damned wagon for the rest of the day. By the time we figured we had been tricked, Buster and Butch would be almost to Denver. We'd have never caught up with them."

"As the bandit told the truth, we'll do it like he said. I know the creek crossing he spoke of. That's where we'll take back your boys, Lark."

"Sure beats riding into town and getting shot at from every door, roof, and window," Moab said from where he was sitting his horse.

"Yeah, Pa," Saul chimed in. "I was having real bad feelings about that too."

Hyrum looked over the waiting men. He hadn't been real eager to hit the town either. Lark was his brother, but Buster and Butch were about as bright as a moonless night. It would have been a real tragedy to get his whole gang shot up while trying to rescue those two witless wonders.

"Let's circle ahead to the river crossing. We'll set up a crossfire and put an end to deputy United States marshal Wes Gavin!"

Chapter Sixteen

Wes drove the wagon and remained vigilant. He had to assume Hyrum would be watching the town. He and his men might come riding out of the trees or open fire from anywhere along the trail. Being a prime target sitting on the wagon seat was not a good feeling.

Latigo stayed alert at his side. The Gentleman Bandit's plan had been to keep the Quinteens from hitting the town. Even if they attacked along the trail, the people of Sunset, especially his son, would be safe.

After three hours, they reached the river crossing. The water was a couple of feet deep and sixty feet across, passable except after a hard rain or when the snowmelt caused it to flood. Wes stopped the team at the river's edge, allowing the horses to drink before crossing. He set the brake and watched for trouble. It wasn't a long wait.

"Raise your hands!" a growling voice commanded. "One move, and you're both dead men!"

Wes swung about and saw five men move out into the open with pistols drawn and aimed at him. From the opposite side of the wagon, another four also appeared from the brush and rocky ground cover.

"Latigo!" Wes snarled. "You dirty, crooked sneak! You set this up!"

The Gentleman Bandit had his gun out, pointing it at Wes. He quickly climbed down, while keeping Wes covered.

"Did you think I was going to rot in prison for the rest of my life?" he shouted. "You're ten kinds of a fool, Gavin. I've been playing you for a sucker since you first got the drop on me."

Wes watched as Latigo backed away from the wagon. The man stepped on the side of a rock and tilted, off balance. It was the opening he needed. Wes drew his gun and fired, all in the same motion.

Latigo realized the marshal was going for his gun and quickly pulled the trigger on his own gun. The two shots rang out simultaneously!

Wes doubled over on the wagon seat and slid down to the floor of the wagon. At the same time, Latigo stumbled backward, his hand to his chest, and fell into the creek. There was no sign of life as his body was slowly swept downstream.

"I'll be damned!" Lark Quinteen exclaimed. "Looks like we owe the old man a debt of thanks." Then he bellowed, "Buster! Butch! Sing out, boys! Your pa is here to set you free!"

The men advanced from either side of the wagon, guns still handy but no longer expecting any trouble.

Suddenly, the canvas from the sides of the covered wagon was thrown open and pulled rapidly up to the top of the wagon by rawhide straps. A half dozen men appeared with guns and drew beads on the Quinteen gang!

"Toss down your guns, or die where you stand!" Wes shouted, having risen up high enough to fire over the sideboards of the wagon. Emmett, Kip, and Scat were ready to shoot on one side, and Glen, Pepper, and Raul on the other.

Hyrum foolishly yelled, "It's a trap!"

Lark panicked on the opposite side from Hyrum and fired a round at the wagon. Two others on his side also began to shoot. Hyrum was trying to decide if they should fight when Saul and Rojas opened fire. Their bullets struck the sides of the wagon, but the walls had been reinforced with thick slabs of wood. It prevented the bullets from penetrating through to the men inside.

The Van Ness riders opened up, and a barrage of gunshots echoed through the valley. Smoke and fire belched from gun muzzles, and lead projectiles tore though human flesh. The Quinteen gang had no cover, while the men in the wagon could shoot from relative safety.

Even as Moab was struck in the leg, Saul was hit in the chest. Sentry had tried to scramble for some rocks, but he was hit in the back. Rojas got off a couple of shots but went down in the first volley of return fire. Lark, who had started the shooting, was hit by no fewer than four bullets.

Hyrum dropped his rifle and whirled about to run for cover, trying to reach the horses. Three or four steps was as far as he got, because a dozen Van Ness riders came pounding down the trail with guns drawn. From across the river, another ten cowboys appeared, mounted on horseback, with rifles cocked and ready to fire. There was nowhere to run, no escape. Hyrum lifted his hands, gritted his teeth, and watched his men being cut down.

Mort and Whitey were in a fight they didn't want and quickly threw away their guns. Hank had been too slow to make up his mind. A bullet in the shoulder made the decision for him, and he was out of the fight. In less than a minute, the skirmish was over.

The Van Ness riders swarmed forward, their guns trained on every member of the Quinteen gang. They quickly disarmed the bunch, and a man or two remained on guard to keep watch on each of the outlaws.

Wes took a moment to check the men in the wagon bed, but no one had been hit. Latigo appeared, thoroughly soaked from floating down the creek. He had a crooked grin on his face and was shaking water from his hat.

"Anyone hurt?" he asked Wes.

"Pepper got a few splinters in one hand, but otherwise we got through without a scratch."

"Good thing you're a good shot," Latigo teased. "I felt the wind of that bullet go by my ear."

"I wanted to make it look good," Wes replied. "I wasn't sure how good an actor you were."

Latigo snorted. "Took a lot more skill for me to sell being shot than you. All you had to do was duck down beneath the wagon seat."

"Yeah? Well, considering how much you talk, my biggest fear was that you might drown. I didn't know if you could keep your mouth shut long enough to be swept down the river and out of the line of fire."

Glen got between them and laughed. "Good thing I know you two are friends. Sound more like a couple of hags fighting over the last hats in the dress shop."

"You know a lot about women's hats, do you?" Latigo turned his attention to Glen.

"Didn't know they had many of those in the casino or out at the ranch," Wes joined in. "Do you suppose he favors the kind decorated with feathers or flowers?"

Glen raised his hands in surrender. "Okay, I see how it is. It's all right for you two to pick on each other, but everyone else should mind his own business."

Wes turned to overseeing the aftermath of the fight. The Quinteen gang's horses were rounded up, and he took inventory. They treated the wounded, but three of the bunch were already dead, and another wouldn't last till they got back to town. For Hyrum and four others, the injuries were not severe. They would be around to make the trip to Denver when the prison wagon came for them and Lark's other two boys.

"You dirty, lying old sot!" Hyrum cried out at Latigo. "You led us into an ambush and then faked shooting the marshal so our guard would be down."

Latigo shrugged. "I'm a gambler at heart. Haven't you ever heard of a bluff?"

"What about Buster and Butch?" Hyrum wanted to know. "Sentry said the jail was empty."

That put a smile on Latigo's face. "We moved them to a smokehouse last night. Don't you worry none, they will be there to share the two cells with you and your pals."

"You better hope I never get free, old man!" Hyrum bellowed. "I'll carve your gizzard for fish bait!"

"Hyrum," Wes interjected, "considering the number of people who have died in your robberies, the only freedom you can look forward to is when death comes calling."

Three men rode in the back of the wagon with the wounded. The dead were draped over their horses, and the remaining trio of Van Ness riders rode back on the other Quinteen mounts. Bound with rope and surrounded by twenty riders, Hyrum and his boys had no chance to try anything cute.

Everyone in Sunset was on the main street when the small army of men returned. It was like a parade. Once the lead Van Ness rider announced that no one from the ranch had been hurt, there was a good deal of cheering.

The captured outlaws were herded into the jail. Shep returned Butch and Buster from the smokehouse, but the family reunion was not a happy one. Lark and three other gang members were dead, and they were all destined for trials in Denver. It was the end of the Quinteen gang.

Dee arrived with notebook and pen in hand. She scribbled a few details about the ambush and then took Emmett along with her to help fill in the blanks for her story.

Ogden had come to town when his riders made their trip to the river. He was standing in front of the jail and greeted his men with a wide smile.

"All Van Ness riders have the rest of the day off," he called to them. "Any food or drink you men consume will be paid for by me. Until midnight, that is," he added with a chuckle. The news brought another round of cheers, mostly from the Van Ness riders.

"However," he added, "I'll expect you all back at the ranch for work tomorrow as usual."

Most of the cowboys headed for the two saloons, while Wes waited for a private moment with Shep and Latigo. As soon as he thanked Ogden for the help of his men, he took the sheriff and the Gentleman Bandit aside.

"Shep," Wes began, "I have to ask a favor from you."

The sheriff wrinkled his brow. "Anything you want, Marshal. You pretty much saved my life and maybe the town as well."

"In the report we send to Denver, concerning the Quinteen gang," he began, "there is one change I want to make." Shep looked at him expectantly, while Latigo only showed a puzzled curiosity. "I need to add one more to the list of those killed in today's fight."

Shep did not hide his surprise. "The fourth Quinteen man died on the way here, and Sentry don't look that bad. I'm pretty sure he'll pull through. The other wounded don't look to be in danger of dying."

"We still need to include one more of the wanted men." He cast a sidelong glance at Latigo. "I need to report that the Gentleman Bandit was killed."

Latigo's mouth fell open in shock. Shep looked sharply at his estranged father and then back at Wes. "You want me to back up a lie?"

"It's no lie," Wes assured him. "The Gentleman Bandit was killed when he fell from a fifty—uh, better make that a hundred-and-fifty-foot—cliff. That was the same day Jack Donahue showed up to save my life, when Buster and Butch got the drop on me."